I0682065

Night
Mara

Romina D'Alessandro

WC B●●KS

This is a work of fiction. Names, characters, businesses, places, events and incidents are either the products of the author's imagination or used in a fictitious manner. Any resemblance to actual persons, living or dead, or actual events is purely coincidental.

Copyright © 2015 Romina D'Alessandro

All rights reserved.

ISBN: 069252326X

ISBN-13: 9780692523261

To Kevin

1

Agoura Hills, CA: if you don't get to the supermarket by midnight, you'll be having a day-old donut for dinner again. Thanks, gas station. When you snap out of a daydream this late, however, you know where the last of your money's going. You need some weed. Not much else can regulate your sleep schedule that quick, and the more you think about it, the more it makes sense. You gotta get hungry somehow too, right? Although if you're trying to get hungry, you need food, whereas sober, you can just wait for the rumbling to pass through your stomach and onto somewhere else, bringing you pain, subsiding eventually after another glass of water. But seeing as you're worrying about the now, how much more into these beats you're creating you could get, the night long ahead of you, you look up what store's delivering at this time and order an eighth for fifty dollars.

It's funny how this town does business, because you can't buy pot at a store, but you can have it delivered to your door. Or the parking structure under your apartment since they're drug dealers after all. Structure D, structure D, the one with the huge D on it, you tell the driver over the phone, but it isn't so obvious to him. By now you think this man might be actually retarded, going up the driveway looking at the first structure, and then the second structure, and then the third structure, and then the fifth structure...D, man, D, like A, B, C, D.

After a while he finds you shivering in the dim fluorescent light as a strange rain drains from the opening of parking structure D and is blown onto your toes. You're not a flip-flop person, but someone has been stealing one sock from your wash ever since you moved here, and yesterday was when the inevitable occurred: there were no more pairs. You figured you'll have to mix socks from now on, but you'll revisit that later. So you grabbed the pair of flip-flops your brother second-handed you about a month ago for no reason when you went to dinner with him and his girlfriend, and hurried out and down the stairs. Somewhere in there beneath duct taped headphones must have been when it started drizzling. Now you have a bottle of green trees and a can of beans, at least, you hope.

On the way out, the headlights of a 2009 Chevy Malibu blindly turn into the garage. A faint rush of panic interrupts Jameson's walk, and he hides the generic paper bag of drugs in his pocket. He stops, then the car stops, and the driver, some frowning middle-aged man he sees from time to time in situations like this one, waves for him to go, so he hurries across to avoid any further trouble, making the slightest eye contact with his female companion.

Almost slipping, Jameson makes it to his apartment in ten seconds. He uses both locks on the door—something he keeps insisting that Artie partake in if she would only remember to—and immediately slips out into the balcony, seeking shelter in the water closet where he keeps his bong. Thunder in the distance, Jameson takes his time with a large bowl. Times of plenty.

"No, what I'm saying is: I need one to get to work, but I need a job to get one, so, like, where do I start, you know?" The somewhat loud whine makes it feel quieter than before. Two people are going up the stairs. The other person doesn't seem to want to discuss this right now, refraining from speaking. "Because I'm telling you, I looked online and the bus routes are shit." There could be children around, ladies, yet this girl gives no fucks. Besides, she's right. She's gonna need a car, and she's very aware of how impossible that is, her tone hopeless, accusing the other person of fault. Metal bangs against the railing as she steps on the landing, following the surer steps of the man, that man Jameson always sees frowning—by the mailboxes, the leasing office, at the gas station even, utterly wretched every time. "They take forever and they stop really early, so unless my hours are between hours that they're not gonna be given the kind of job I'm suited to do, it's gonna be fucking dandy."

"Mel," the man breaks his silence, his voice obscenely demanding like what Jameson expected, "watch the negative attitude."

Without noticing he's doing it, Jameson sets the bong down and exits his hiding spot to look in the direction of the last apartment on the opposite end where the man, wearing a satisfying frown, gets the key in the lock and twists the knob open. He goes inside before the girl and this annoys her, especially since she's carrying a ton of crap. What did he even mean by his comment anyway? She's confronting an irritating reality.

As she fumbles with two suitcases and a large comforter as well as a backpack and a laptop case, Jameson wonders what she could have done to offend the man into treating her with such disrespect. Men, he figures.

He exhales disapprovingly and turns on his heels, eyeing the foggy moon calmly under a good high. When he finds himself the most amount of wet he can handle before feeling uncomfortable, he aims for the door, except he's once again distracted by these people when the girl storms out of the apartment, head bowed, step steady, down to retrieve more things from the car. Jameson hears her get to it, unlock it, load up, lock it, and then sees the top of her head emerge from below.

"Need any help?" he asks.

She doesn't look up right away, so startled she has to gather herself before turning around.

"Oh, no. Thanks," she adds awkwardly, her voice deeper than before.

She struggles with a hefty crate of records taking one step, then another, her fingers crushed under the plastic's hard edges.

"No, no," he resists, automatically flip-flopping out of his apartment and down the stairs to help her before she can make any meaningful movements, not thinking clearly, just thinking fast. "These things are a bitch. Let me help you."

"Oh, well, thanks."

He takes the crate from her hands easily and parades his strength by remaining idly behind her so she may show the way, now carrying nothing but a light tote bag, making her feel useless.

"Are you moving or—"

"Yeah," she answers, her face bleary from hours of travel-ing. "Yeah."

"Welcome to the neighborhood then. I'm Jameson."

He stops, repositioning his grip on the crate onto his left hand to give her his right one. She thinks before shaking it.

"Mel."

"Yeah, I heard." She looks sideways. "I mean, your...was that your...dad..."

"Yeah."

"Yeah, he just mentioned it and I happened to hear it."

"So you didn't mean to be weird."

"No, no, I would never."

"Good."

She gets to the door and opens it, steps in, looks at Jameson, extends her hands, takes the crate, and smiles one last time, mumbling her thanks before nervously closing the door.

"So where'd you move from? No? Okay."

Jameson is taken aback, but it's simply too early to make an assessment. He makes his way out of the off-putting interaction, returning to his own loneliness. The first thing he'll do is wash his feet and put socks on. One of these days he'll have to visit Ross to get a dozen.

Mel doesn't move until she thinks she's heard him close his door. At least she can't hear him talking to himself anymore.

"I don't want you leaving anything in the car overnight," her dad almost snaps, already in the old shorts and T-shirt he wears to bed.

"I'll get it out," she hisses back.

With newfound vigor, she takes the records to the guest bedroom. She'll only need one more trip to the Malibu, but she'd rather wait until she's sure the neighbor won't come out to help her again, probably some time in the AM. It's not like her exhaustion could be readily relieved with sleep. Readjusting to a whole new place takes time. If the conditions agree with her, maybe in a week she'll be able to poop here, and that's all she can ask for.

"That's Grandpa's," she states, pointing at the record player shoved in a corner next to the mirrored doors of the closet.

Holding a glass of water, Herman looks in her direction from the kitchen.

"Yes, yeah. For you. He said he remembered how much you liked it when you were over last time, and he wanted you to make some good use of it."

"Yeah, I know. Just confirming."

"You talked to Johnny?"

"No, Mom talked with Grandma."

5

"She did?"

"Yeah, chill, dude. That's why I brought my mom's old records."

"Don't start hoarding stuff."

Dragging her feet, Mel closes the door, leaving Herman to his thoughts. He doesn't have many, yet he manages to remember to take his medicine with the glass of water he's already poured. Before going to bed, he rejoices once more in that his daughter is home, knocking on Mel's door and whispering: "Good night."

She gives him a monotone, "You too," which probably pleases him, and goes back to figuring out everything from scratch, her belongings all on the floor, the few pieces of furniture waiting to be used, walls bare, carpet clean. Herman hasn't said anything about what he was using the room for prior to her move. It made little sense for someone so miserly to get an apartment bigger than he had use for, but when Mel needed a place to crash, Dad was there with an empty room.

It's all too good to be true, she knows it. That's why she's not even excited. She's gone through the process every couple of years most of her life. When she's about to die/murder from living with her mother all year, she can flee to Dad's a few hours away. After some family bonding, enough to make up for lost time, Mel gladly crawls back to Mom. The cycle repeats itself.

Now it's been three years since her last visit, and the milestones father and daughter have compiled have only been acknowledged over one-sentence text messages. He got divorced, did a bad investment, and lost forty pounds. She dropped out of college, quit smoking cigarettes, and attempted suicide. Not all bad, as you can see. Still recuperating one day at a time, somehow this new arrangement is supposed to help. Mel's mom gave her a hundred dollar bill making her promise she would keep it with her at all times in case she desperately needed it for some reason. Expectations are low.

To stay occupied, there's a psychiatrist appointment to prepare for and a gym membership to get—and, ugh, use— both to be paid by her mom through PayPal transfers. After that, Mel will have to start looking for a job, then she'll have to land one, and ultimately she'll have to avoid getting fired. None of these last three things has she ever tried in her twenty-one years of age. When she thinks about it, her heart pumps a venomous batch of blood that instantly cools her body, reheats it again, and eventually nears fainting, gasping one last time. What she's been up to all this time, she has no idea.

Opening her bags reveals little of her personality besides the fact that she's a lazy dresser, a sign of being a lazy person. She had wanted to leave as much as possible behind, but her mom convinced her to bring a few things. Like a scarf. She isn't gonna need one. She didn't need one in Riverside, and she doesn't need one in Ventura. Still the damned thing made it all the way here on the train, impossibly distressing a trip with her large cargo, which she had to endure because the thought of picking her up ninety miles away was insulting to Herman.

A buzzing builds in Mel's pocket, erupting in a pretty dope synthesizer until she picks up.

"Hey," she drags offbeat.

"What's up?" asks Rodrigo, her kind-of boyfriend, on the other end. "How did the trip go?"

"It was fine. I don't think I lost anything." Mel kicks off her Converse and throws herself on the brand new mattress, bouncing off it for a second or two. "This mattress feels pretty nice."

"Cool."

"Yeah, I used to sleep on the sofa bed at his other house. It was cool 'cause I had the TV. But, like, I have my own room and everything. It's pretty rad, I guess."

"That sounds great."

"Meh, you know?" she switches ears, looking for a pillow. "Like...I dunno yet. My grandparents have always lived really close to here and it's not in any way...fun. But I guess it's close to L.A. Closer. When he used to live in Santa Monica, that...that was cool. But maybe this is good now."

"Quieter?"

"Yeah, like, shit, I dunno, maybe I'm just going from one hell hole to another. We went out to dinner downtown, and we also went grocery shopping around there 'cause he was saying the stores close really early out here. And then we were stuck in traffic even though it's super late. I just got here. I seriously just put down the crate of records. This neighbor dude had to help me. My dad's such a dick."

"You couldn't carry them yourself?"

Mel ignores this question and gets on her feet, walking towards the closet. She opens it, making sure to not get her fingers on the mirror, and merrily finds two pillows on the shelf, unopened purple Ikea bed sheets, and a small amount of hangers.

"Tomorrow I bet my grandparents are gonna come over, or we're gonna go to their house. One or the other. The record player's here, by the way. It's gonna be awesome. I just gotta figure out how to connect it or even where to put it. I'm gonna have to get a dresser or something. A little table or..."

Using her teeth, she rips the sheets' packaging open, putting the phone between her shoulder and ear to unfold the contents. Though she tries, she can't do both.

"Well, I just wanted to call to make sure everything's good."

"Everything's good. You can go to sleep."

"Gotta wake up early tomorrow."

"Work?"

"Yeah. Talk to you later."

"Nite, nite."

He hangs up first. Leaving the phone on the desk, Mel goes ahead and makes the bed like she's antsy to. She takes the comforter she brought along and—though it must have definitely gotten pretty dirty—places it neatly atop the twin bed. The pillows go in the cases, the opening facing the wall, just the way she likes it, and after taking off her jeans, she lays. Her eyes close for a moment, deciding how snug the new setting is. Not too shabby. Incomparable to her room in her mom's house where she enjoys a queen-sized bed with the most modern mattress technology for her pains, a two hundred dollar body pillow at the ready, but Mel's an adaptable, grateful lass just as long as she isn't being an intolerant brat.

Though she had expected to be so bored in her insomnia that putting her stuff away would keep her entertained all night—a pile of shit here, a pile of shit there—a quick look in the medicine cabinet during a trip to the bathroom proves to put a sure end to her plans.

"Diazepam," she reads under her breath, a grin spreading across her somber face. Not so aloof anymore, she pops three pills without checking the milligrams. Rock and roll.

It reminds her to take the rest of her meds, and they get stuck in her throat while she figures out her father's drinking water system—Brita pitcher, of course. Wondering whether it's still raining, she looks through the blinds and finds the outside wet but serene. Immediately regretting getting cozy, she remembers there's still stuff in the car. Sighing, she gets her jeans and sneakers back on before grabbing the keys from the counter and going out. She looks in all directions to make sure no one's there. Not that she disliked the fellow. She's just not a people person. It's a mystery how she plans on making friends. As she reaches the dark grey Malibu, it occurs to her that perhaps she already soiled what could have turned into a beautiful friendship. He had eyed her copy of *Ram*, she knew it. She made sure to pay attention to that.

Mel takes a grocery bag in one hand and a jug of orange juice in her pinky before closing the trunk with a heavy, heavier than usual push. It wasn't the door that was weighty, it was her thrust. She giggles, the wet footprints she left on her way there guiding her through the structure. Trying to not do anything stupid, she quickens her no-gravity walk, passing Jameson's apartment noisily half on purpose, half on Valium. After much decision-making, she uses both locks on the door thanks to a little paranoia, certain it's still best to take precaution. The bedroom door happens to have a lock too, so that one gets turned as well. Although something could happen to her, especially now, so no, no, undo the lock. Make sure it's undone. Open, close. Yeah.

Privacy begins subduing her, the bed calling, but the voice that's still harder than this to shut up comes up with a great idea. Why not write Jameson a letter? A note. A note saying: *Dear Jameson, nice meeting you. Sorry I was weird. I wasn't feeling too hot. I'm new and I don't know anyone, so let's be friends. Sincerely, Mel.* All right, a letter.

But no, she laughs, the pencil rolling off the desk. She takes the green sticky note and holds it proudly in the lamp's light. It's the worst idea she's ever had since the love letter she sent to Warren Foster the summer after seventh grade because she thought she was moving and never coming back to her school. Of course it turned out to be one of her parents' normal freak-outs and not something real, thus Mel didn't move in with her dad and had to return in the fall to see Warren Foster opening his locker. Mel avoided him at all costs, but he was truly a gentleman. They never talked about it, he didn't tell anyone, and they managed to have normal conversations in front of other people for the remainder of middle school. Bless him.

Staring at it, she reads the note one more time. Still finding it hilarious, she puts it in her pocket and proceeds to take off her jeans, which is harder over the shoes. She must go through the whole process of noticing it'd be easier if she took those off first, which takes her a while.

The more she fights the feeling, the more nauseated she becomes, but it's very inconvenient how none of her things are easy to get to. She wants to change her socks, brush her hair, brush her teeth, brush away the day, her head resting on the purple pillowcase, the neighbor with his light on. What if he was also bored? But she, she shouldn't be bored, and so she flings her arm through the stuffy air and unzips the laptop bag to get to her headphones, plugs them into her cell phone, and you know what, she's gonna give that album Rodrigo keeps talking about a chance. How bad could it be? New town, new music, new friends, new fucking life, man. New fucking life.

2

Slightly more conscious by the second as light enters the room, Mel isn't aware of it yet, but this is one of the best sleeps she's ever had. It tangos with death so delicately that you just want more to finally be done with it.

Going for the right middle finger he chews on on the regular since his adolescence—disgusting, knobby little thing—Herman keeps trying to decide what to do even though he's already decided. That's his problem, but he's about to fix it. He starts by walking away from Mel, vomit hanging from her mouth across and down the bed. Some of it has gotten on her hair, forehead, tip of her nose, but the angelic, drunken look on her face remains. She doesn't stink of alcohol or anything, and despite not wanting to notice this, he can tell she threw up the tuna melt sandwich she got with him the night she arrived. It's now been two days of this, and he doesn't necessarily know how to go about it.

On Saturday, his parents called to say they were coming, but Herman advised them against it. "I don't know if she'll be awake by the time you get here," he insisted. They were simply too eager to understand. "And she needs to sleep. One of the things she struggles with the most is not being able to, so now that she can, she has to. It must be the mattress."

They agreed, but Sunday comes and they're calling again. He ignores the call, filling a glass with water. His knees crack and his socks make a rasping sound against the linoleum floor. They must be getting old. Estimating how long they can still last him, he cracks and rasps towards what is now Mel's room and kneels in front of her. Hanging from a chord, Mel's cell phone has run out of battery playing *Salad Days* from start to finish over and over again. A tiny snore escapes her confused sinus cavity. That's when Herman dips his fingers in the water and sprinkles them over his daughter's face. Her mouth closes and the tongue sticks to the palate, making it click. He does it one more time.

"Mel—Melaina? Melaina."

He grabs her shoulder and shakes it a bit. She whispers a groan and rubs her open mouth dry on her arm. Herman insists on the shoulder shaking to make sure she doesn't drift back asleep. Suddenly she opens her eyes, closes them against her will, and tries hard to see, the blinds open all the way, contrasting to the coma-like experience of, in other words, overdosing.

"What?" is all she can ask.

"Good afternoon," he says almost soothingly.

"Hi."

Sitting up, Mel attempts to make sense of what she remembers. It isn't much. At one point the ceiling dumped low on her and the bedding absorbed what squeezed through the pores...

"You okay?" A disoriented look crosses her eyes, and she nods. "You hungry?" he asks, unsure why that's important with so many other questions left.

13

She shakes her head all the way to the shoulder, and he thinks she wants to discretely smell her armpits. It's a good thing she doesn't. The perspiration is shiny on her face, brown tresses stuck to her temples coming from the opposite ends of her head. And of course, there's the vomit. It takes her perhaps too long to notice it, but when she does, she has a hard time making peace with it, though she does. With the setting clearer, Mel takes a deep breath.

"What time is it?"

Barely checking his watch, Herman responds: "Two thirty. Sunday," he adds, watching her expression alter only by a hair of surprise.

"I'm gonna take a shower."

The father gets back into a firm stance, feeling like he dealt with the happenstance more than nicely. It doesn't feel finished, however, so when she runs off into the bathroom, he doesn't know what to do with his hands. Trying to fill them, he goes on to make scrambled eggs.

Crystalline sunlight hits through the gambrel roofs of the building complex in hostile angles, and this shines through the tall bathroom window onto Mel's brow as she pees. There're no regrets, not even now in the puke reek, the chagrin, none.

After throwing her clothes into a corner, she takes a semi-cold shower, neglecting her hair because Herman's bald and she forgot to bring in the grocery bag with the toiletries. Her body receives the fresh start it needs and that's what matters. She finishes quickly. The shower head drips due to her ignorance of it requiring a more solid turn. Drips and drips. Eventually she notices but does nothing about it.

Straight back to her room, Mel fails to recognize the smell of breakfast being served. Herman gives her five minutes before knocking. Standing there with a spatula, it feels like ten.

"Just a second," she responds with her meds in her mouth, coming out. "Yeah?"

"I made you some eggs."

"Oh. Thank you."

She sits down at the table, burying the necessity to bring up the fact she had mentioned she wasn't hungry. He has already eaten, but he makes sure to serve himself a small cup of coffee to accompany her.

"So what…" he presses on. "What happened to you?"

"What do you mean?"

"You know, sleeping like that. Was dinner that bad or—"

"I guess. I dunno. It happens sometimes."

"What do you mean?"

"When I'm exhausted, I just pass out for however long I need to recover."

"But I thought you were having trouble sleeping."

"Yeah, well, I wouldn't call this paradise," she says, almost mocking him.

"So you just have sleeping…problems?"

"I just can't sleep right, no matter what I do."

"That…wow, that…"

"Yeah, it sucks."

"I'm the same way, don't get me wrong."

"I know."

"For me it's that I'm a light sleeper. I'm always waking up for one reason or another. Either a noise or to go to the bathroom, always something," he lingers on.

"That's rough."

"Yes. Yes, it is."

Mel takes a large bite, and when she becomes aware of the mixture falling apart in her mouth, she gags unnoticeably, swallowing the thing whole, chasing it with orange juice till there's none left in the glass. Herman watches her and thinks this is what a hungry child looks like.

"Could you help me connect the speakers later?" she asks to fill the silence, the TV off, no music playing, all very adult-like depleted of life.

"Sure."

He takes his finger to his teeth while staring at the light bulb's reflection in his coffee. He drinks it, licking his lips at the end, savoring the lasting taste of skin on his crooked central incisors. Mel's teeth are fucked up in the same exact fashion, like both their nails square off elegantly on their fingers and toes, and how their eyebrows are thickly shaped but their eyelashes lack in lush. Besides that, there's little resemblance.

Not wanting to take her time, Mel absentmindedly shoves the rest of her food down her throat, trying to figure out where she's gonna get her daily dose of marijuana from now on in this town. Her previous plan of leaving that lifestyle behind her is evidently not going to work out. There's the anorexia, anxiety, insomnia. She needs it. Some people just need it.

"I'm gonna go for a walk," she says, getting up with her plate to take it to the sink.

"Around the neighborhood?"

"Nah, just the complex. Learn where everything is, you know?"

"Oh, yeah, sure."

She leaves the plate and fills it with water, looking at her dad.

"Can I borrow your keys?"

"Actually," he says, standing up himself. "I made you a copy."

He extracts a silver key on a flimsy ring from the junk drawer. Mel's plan of taking the car key to get a copy is cut short. Not that it would have worked anyway. Instead, she takes the one Herman gives her and puts on her Converse before embarking on a journey down the hill.

She follows the lettering on the buildings atop the garage entrances against alphabetical order, lead by stairs to the pool and barbeque area, then the mailboxes, and finally the leasing office. It has a deck she figures she could hang out at late alone with a joint. Argh, where's she gonna get any, dammit! She can't afford to get a rec.

An old man in a tracksuit walks in her direction where she loiters by a golf cart. When he nears her, she smiles to be polite, but the old man ignores her, his glower full of bad vibes. Well, he can go fuck himself.

She goes to the mailboxes, questioning whether her dad didn't make her a copy of the mailbox key on purpose or if he forgot, because she's gonna want one. Used to the middle of nowhere as she is, all her possessions are purchased online. And Rodrigo said he'd send a letter, probably a postcard, though nothing really. She should expect nothing.

Thinking of him, she checks her phone. As she should have expected. Her friends also seem to have forgotten about her big move, if she even told them. It's hard to keep up with that's truly important as the years go by.

"Hey!"

Mel raises her head in the direction of the driveway and sees a fatigued Jameson biking slowly on his way back from wherever he was. He's got a backpack on, his hair sweating the gel off, pulling a water bottle from the holder as he makes up his mind to bike to her. She waits impatiently twisting on her ankles.

"Hello," she says as he gets closer.

"What's up? Just got outta work. Had this stupid breakfast party I had to wake up for. And then my car wouldn't start...but

I shouldn't brag. How are you? Getting your mail for the first time?" he goes through in a split second.

"No, I don't have a key."

"Yeah, that makes it harder."

"You getting yours?"

"I could. I mostly just wanted to say hi."

She simpers, half lifting her hand to her chest with a wee wave. Jameson jumps off the seat and rolls the bicycle from the handlebars to rest on a trashcan as he looks for his keys in his backpack.

"Nice shirt." This causes him to inspect his torso: Queens of the Stone Age. "I have the same one."

"No way," he says, trying to hide the excitement.

"Yeah, so...I have kind of a weird question to ask you," she blurts out, quick and to the point.

"Go ahead."

"You're a cool dude, right?" she hesitates.

"Is that your question?"

"Ha. I—I'm looking for something."

"Oh."

"Yeah?"

"What, uh..." he mumbles, fumbling with his keys endlessly. "What kinda something?"

"Just weed, man."

"What?! You're asking me for drugs?!"

"I—"

"I'm just fucking with you. Yeah, for sure. You know, you're pretty blunt," he enunciates with a wink, "for being shy."

"Ha, well, gotta get ahead somehow."

"How much do you want?"

"Oh, I dunno, however much...I mean, I'm gonna need it, like, from now on."

"I have a card, it's all good."

"Well, now could I get maybe a joint or two?"

"A joint or two?" He opens the mailbox and checks its empty contents, closing it back up. "I don't think the mailman's come yet."

"It's Sunday, isn't it?"

"Well, there you go."

"But yeah, the thing is: I didn't bring a piece. Thought I would stop. But it's been one day...two? And I'm already going crazy so...anyway, how much would that be?"

"Okay," he starts, putting his hands before him to grasp her question before he can forget. "I'll give you a joint for free if you're willing to share it with me." She avoids his stare, fixated on the floor. "Unless you're busy and you need it, I mean, I'll sell it to you, no problem."

"No, I...I'm down. Totally. I...dude, I need friends just as much. If not more."

"That's what I like to hear. Are you free right now? I smoke as soon as I get home."

"Uh, yeah. Of course."

He scratches the bottom of his shoe against the ground, waiting for her to show to be sure. When he sees her eyelids close and long away from him into the sky, he begins inching towards his apartment. A half step off rhythm, Mel follows scared, everything she ever believed in concerning safety not as important anymore.

Once Jameson opens the door, she lets down her guard at the sight of a fully furnished, pretty clean abode. It stinks a little bit of cigarettes, but it's faint, no ashtray visible.

"What do you drink?" he asks, turning on the kitchen light.

"Oh, I don't really do that."

"You don't get thirsty?" he makes fun, opening the fridge and taking out a bottle of grape juice to pour himself a glass.

"I mean alcohol."

"I know. Yeah, I'm not a big drinker either. I don't even have any booze to offer you, so good thing that was your answer. But I got grape juice. You want grape juice?" he asks, reaching for another glass.

"I'm not sure if I like grape juice."

"You'll love it," he insists.

He rapidly gives it to her so she may not protest or think about the taste of something unknown, which grosses out the majority of people, before going past her into his bedroom, the same one as Mel's only mirrored. She understands this as an invitation, but she remains in the living room trying to decipher, given the sounds, what he's doing in there. It doesn't take him long to find what he's looking for, and the self-titled Queens of the Stone Age begins spinning on a turntable.

"Since you like 'em," he says, coming back out. "Here," he touches her arm, pointing her in the right direction, "I always smoke in the water closet."

He opens the door of the balcony, guiding her into the teeny space where his bong awaits. He takes out a canister from his pocket and packs a bowl. Mel reminds herself to breathe through her nose when the room starts getting smaller. Jameson looks at the closed door, and she thinks she catches the same look in his eyes that she must be having. Without thinking much about it, she turns the knob and the door pulls away a good five inches on its own. The both of them take one long breath through their mouths, blinking at the time of exhaling. The airflow increases and that seems to do the trick. Jameson pulls out a lighter and hands it to her.

"Greens?"

"Heck yeah," she whisper-yells, finding herself stupid for saying that in the tone she did. This guy doesn't know her. He might judge her. She must redeem herself. Her brain reaches into its nothingness, hoping to find something worthwhile. "So how long have you been living here?"

"Four, five months."

"How do you like it?"

"It's, uh...it sucks honestly."

"How?"

"As soon as we moved in, we had to basically pack everything up again because it got infested with cockroaches. Little ones everywhere in the kitchen. And just a few days before, the people underneath us had moved, so clearly they let the roach problem get to that point and it just—ah," he sighs. "It was really frustrating."

"Fuck, yeah, man, I'm sorry."

She takes another large hit and chases it with grape juice. He finishes the bowl and softly pushes the door open with his fingers, forcing Mel to take a few steps backward or he'll invade her personal space, puddles from last night's rain left on the balcony where the uneven flooring shows its vulnerability.

"Yeah, there's a whole lotta small things that just add up and—ugh. Honestly, I'm just waiting till I have some money saved up to get the hell outta here."

"It's great to hear that now that I just moved in. Who...who do you live with?"

"My friend Artie," he tells her. "Roommates and band mates."

"Oh, cool. What's it called?"

"The band?"

"No, the sitcom you guys are in."

"Ha," he kinda laughs. "Night Mara."

"Huh. That's not bad. But I feel like..." He lowers a brow, lifts the other, just as Mel feels a sinus headache coming on, the price she pays. "No? No, I guess it's...it's just one of those, you know? It sounds like it's already a thing. Because it's so good, I mean. It's a compliment."

"Thanks. I didn't come up with it."

"Artie?"

"Yeah. But I love everything it stands for. It's like nightmare, it's a weird-ass animal, it's a demon, it means bitter, and I love Rooney Mara. At least that's my interpretation. I don't know where she got it from."

"Maasai Mara."

"It's just such a pretty name."

"Mara Salvatrucha."

"Makes it sound harmless."

"My ex step sister's name was...well, technically she was Isamara."

Jameson seems pleased with himself as he gallantly asks Mel to go back inside. This time she goes into his bedroom right behind him. There's not much there: a queen-sized inflatable mattress with too many mismatching blankets rolled into one ball, a record player, a bunch of speakers, an acoustic guitar, an electric guitar, and two crates full of records amongst cables and notebooks and stained white T-shirts scattered almost out of view in a corner.

"Sorry it's so messy."

"That's sick," she says, pointing at a charcoal drawing of Kurt Cobain in a half-broken glass frame.

"My friend's friend drew it. You like Nirvana?"

"Dude, I grew up on Nirvana. My babysitter got fired because she would play her *Nevermind* cassette like a maniac. I would nap to it."

"You must be fucked up. But at least it wasn't *In Utero.*"

Mel laughs through her nose, discreetly wiping it on her T-shirt when he's not looking. They both contemplate whether Jameson's comment was appropriate, something that solely depends on their personal understandings of mental illness itself. Mel presses her lips together to keep herself from defending suicide. Jameson wonders where he stands today on the murder conspiracies he's studied throughout the years. Sitting on the mattress, he grabs the closest notebook and proceeds to roll a joint, a process that takes him too much time to Mel's standards but especially her patience.

Chatty as he fancies himself, Jameson respects Mel's preference for silence in favor of savoring the rich sound of one of his favorite records.

"It's great," she lets him know at the same exact moment it crosses his mind. "I inherited my mom's old records, so I have nothing like this. Mostly Beatles. Some Creedence. Elton."

"Moms love Elton John."

"And the Bee Gees."

"That," he chuckles. "Yup."

And she starts to pace. She's always pacing. On the phone, brushing her teeth, thinking, thinking, thinking a lot, too much, sit down to calm down, and then when you realize it, you're on your feet again without meaning to just pacing, still pacing. Staring at her shoes, she stops, the inertia of the upper half of her body making her look even kookier. But Jameson doesn't notice this. What he does see is that, curved and unappealing on the mattress as he is, there's no proper place for her to sit.

"You can, uh, sit there if you like," he tells her, his hand motioning to a large subwoofer. "It's broken."

Mel tests the surface with her hand. Pretty stable, though it does make her feel fat when, upon sitting on it, she must now preoccupy herself with not applying her whole weight, hanging on with both feet planted firmly. She swallows except she can't, taking the glass of grape juice to her lips. First she wets them, then she opens her mouth. The gulp extends to the back of the throat, and Jameson could swear she swishes the mixture ere swallowing. Her smile lengthens with two purple lines up her cheeks. Trying not to, she feels overwhelmingly observed.

"Cotton mouth," she explains when she catches him looking.

"Oh. Yeah. Same. So where'd you move from?"

Either they get to know each other till the end, or at a certain point they'll grow bored of each other's me-me-me. So far in the you-you-you, what when where who why and how, they have scarce information to be sharing germs. And on that note, Jameson lifts the joint, spinning it to catch every imperfection, deciding it's good enough.

"Riverside."

"That's not too far, is it?"

Shrugging, Mel tells him that, "It all depends on your perception."

"A friend of mine lives there. Anthony, you know him?"

"Well..."

"I'm just kidding. It's 'cause he's black, so you know how white people always assume...never mind."

"No, I get it. It'd be funnier if I was black."

"Yeah, probably. He goes to UCR. Anthony Morris."

"No, dude, I don't know him," she coughs.

He gets up, his lower back radiating the cold-hot pain of sleeping near the ground, and waves the thin joint in front of Mel's face. She nods enthusiastically, and that's so gratifying his lips curve upward, an expression he's not used to, leading her back to the balcony. This time Jameson shakes his head at the water closet and pulls out two lawn chairs to unfold, placing them each before the round, somewhat still wet table. What's with him and sitting all the time?

"Thank you," she says, her leg going up and down, up and down, anything in contact with anything in contact with her rattling just as much.

Jameson lights the joint and works his way around getting it to burn evenly. It takes him about four hits. Mel, who has been counting, puff puffs twice.

She won't stay long, she's decided. There's stuff she needs to do. Now all she has to do is come up with a good way to put it. Like, 'thanks for the bud, I'm out,' would not be her most dignified.

"I'm postponing the unpacking aspect of this whole ordeal," she says dehydrated, sipping.

He agrees, ashing out of the balcony railing. A neighbor underneath them sees this and goes berserk rather quickly though quietly, dragging on her dog's leash sharply back on home.

"I hate all the fucking dogs," he contemplates.

"Don't tell me you're a cat person."

"No pets. No fucking pets."

"I always found it kinda evil how people in apartments have 'em."

"These people here, oh, you don't even know. They jack off to their dogs. It's disturbing. My roommate, she has a little fucking Chihuahua. Celeste," he derides. "Most retarded thing in the world. It just sits on her bed all day depressed as fuck, barking at me whenever I'm near, and sometimes I go just to say hey, see what it's up to. Being miserable, it's all it knows. But then when Artie comes home, the dog is finally alive. It stands on its hind legs and does a dance and shit. It's ridiculous. So then Artie has no idea how fucking suicidal that dog is when she's not around. And I mean it when I say it. Once I found it inside a huge plastic bag. That was when we had just moved. Just sitting there dying. So I call Artie, she flips a shit, hurries home, and when she gets here, the dog's doing the fucking Macarena."

"Is it here?" Mel asks after a pause.

"Yeah," he says, catching his breath, looking at the roach he's holding before tossing it in the ashtray. "Come here," and as he stands up, when his back is turned, Mel pockets what remains of the joint.

Mel follows Jameson in and across the living room where the larger bedroom begins. She hasn't even been this far into her own apartment. Shadows begin forming as Jameson gently reveals the mess, natural light coming in through the half open window, hitting bits and pieces of silk, velvet, leather, lace, denim on every possible surface. Atop this mountain of color, enclosed within a tulle canopy, a single pathetic animal, its face void.

"I see what you mean," she says.

"Yup."

"It's a piece of shit."

"It really is. But hey," he warns, "not a word of this to Artie. She'd disown me."

"I don't even know her."

"But you will. You will. She leaves for a day or two. Comes back all hungover."

"And she left the dog? You feed it while she's gone, right?"

Jameson' eyes widen, every muscle flexes. When did Artie leave again?

"She usually takes it with...she must have gotten mat at it, punishing it. Artie can be pretty mean."

Feeling like she doesn't want to deal with the conversation that follows, Mel turns her head, her mouth half open, spiritless. There's a few wispy grey hairs on a spot on the back of her head. He thinks about the few red hairs coming from his stubble, the rest thick black.

"And on that note, I think I gotta head back. Got lots to do," she lets him know.

"Do you want a joint to take home?" he asks, his eyes twinkling in the kitchen light. It convinces Mel to leave faster.

"It's cool. Even this awesome L.A. shit doesn't get me that high these days," she blabbers, walking in reverse. "I'll catch you later."

Her will is beyond what he can control, and she dashes away stealthily with not a simple goodbye, the fact that he couldn't help her with his drugs also making him feel bad. 'Me too,' he was ready to say, or, 'Me neither,' can't remember which. But it was gonna be a revelation, and she didn't care to stay.

Mel checks her phone on her way back to the apartment. No one's been missing her, but she goes ahead and admits to her weaknesses and drafts Rodrigo a text. By the third time she reads it, locking her bedroom door, she decides it's not worth sending. Instead, she sends him a fine *whachoo up to?* and waits. And waits.

It takes hours to get a response though the message was received instantly. Sometimes it takes Rodrigo that long to come up with *nuffin muffin*. His behavior is most amusing. After negating her from the start—something Mel doesn't take lightly—he must insist on a conversation, sending a series of stupid thoughts: *i was playing mario kart, drunk mario kart,* and *i'm drunk.*

"Ugh," Mel gargles, her mouth full of cake and Coke, the heartache nearing heartburn.

Grandpa Johnny is sitting on the couch watching the game, Herman unwillingly keeping score while at the same time listening to Grandma Lisa tell Mel about her hip surgery in case she begins to bore or gore her. But Mel's face remains stoic, blinking sporadically behind her glasses as Grandma gets passionate about how intense it all was using florid words like 'tormented' and 'irremediable.' Mel nods a few times, then utters the sounds of amazement, her eyelashes batting in a perfected friendly act. As much as she tries to concentrate on the blood and metal plates and ointments, her mind is freaking out about all the things that cross her mind every five seconds: is she a good person, does good exist, what would it take to make her act on her evil urges, etcetera, etcetera.

This has been going on for the past hour, the Ikea kitchen clock sometimes ticking a second too loud, agitating Mel's lack of concentration. Grandma Lisa eyes her wondering if she's okay. Mel stares on, gulping down more soda. Grandpa Johnny moves his legs and they all look in the direction of the TV as if that meant something's going down. Growing self-conscious, Grandpa Johnny crosses his arms and grunts nonsense like he does. He's probably been wearing the same brown cardigan for the last twenty years. Herman could swear it was thirty.

When Grandma and Grandpa arrived, Mel made sure to thank Grandpa for the stereo and Grandma for the bed sheets. "Beautiful color," she said to Grandma's delight. "Dad still has to help me set it up," she mentioned to Grandpa. Everyone was grateful and in a good mood and everything was great.

Except then it stayed the same, nothing changed, and Herman began to pace, and then Mel went to the bathroom twice without needing to, and they started yawning, contagious one to the other, cooperating unknowingly into getting Grandma and Grandpa to leave.

"They want us gone, Lisa," says Grandpa Johnny with his hands in his pockets.

"All right, good night then," Grandma Lisa says, feeling unloved. She blames her son by forgetting to hug him goodbye. "See you soon, Melaina."

They leave and the living room fills with air. Herman's shoulders loosen and dance up and down in victory. He waits for Mel to initiate conversation, but all she does is wait around until she seems in the clear to go lock herself in her room.

Herman sits down and changes the channel, looking for a documentary or the like, easy enough to catch half-way into it if it came to that. The programming goes from one sport to the next, but he's never been one to go for that. Any time his buddies ever invited him to get wasted and watch a match, he always had something better to do. Even as a young man, he preferred hanging out with his girlfriend, who at the time happened to be Mel's mother. He must have been really under her claw to enjoy being with her more than anything. He couldn't have been himself at the time. Maybe now he would enjoy the atmosphere of a sports bar. Maybe that's what it's all about. Then again, Laura's gone, and that makes a man feel stupid sometimes. The presence of another woman in the house keeps him in check. Now he speculates what kind of woman Mel's turned out to be. He might not be ready to find out.

He comes across an episode of *Cops* and leaves the remote on the other side of the couch, proceeding to chew on his finger, his vision focused solely on the TV. Think about the cameraman. Always think about the cameraman.

Through the wall, Mel dumps out all the contents of her purse and finds the purple lighter she was looking for. She'll be really bummed out when this one gives out. Rodrigo wrote *betch* on it with whiteout, and apparently she finds that sweet.

Mel checks to make sure everything's ready, the door and its lock turned. She opens the window, looks again, and lights the roach she took earlier. She'll just hit it once or twice, leaving the rest for later when she needs to go to sleep. Hopefully tomorrow her new psychiatrist can help her out with that.

Is she nervous? I mean, yeah, a little bit. Who wouldn't be? But this time she'll take it seriously. She won't lie. That's something. Huge, actually. She's gonna be totally and completely honest about the answers to the usual questions. From the sex to the drugs and even bring up some possible childhood traumas because why not, they could point us in the right direction. Sure, it's not therapy, but it's the next best thing. Once she gets a job, she can go to a proper shrink. She remembers a time when her father urged to get her into the hands of psychologists so much that he even paid for it. Those days are gone. By now if it hasn't fixed her, nothing will. Maybe pills, unorthodox to the Nicchi style, but even he is taking all different kinds. The fact that it's a secret makes no difference.

As for her part, Mel has always played little in it. At times she found the resources useful and cried a tear or two in public—her biggest sin, a damn shame—but for the most part, she found it useless.

"I don't know what else I can do," she said a month short of turning eighteen, her heavy backpack still around one arm on the couch. "I feel like I'm gonna be like this for the rest of my life."

The therapist said it didn't have to be that way. All she had to do was change the way she saw the world. It all depends on one's perception, you see. So she went out to the desert and tried to find god. It was the name she gave this purpose, this meaning a human being needs to have in order to get out of bed, if not in the morning, then at night when everyone else is sleeping, when one can be at ease. The smallest piece of heaven, the light at the end of the tunnel during a dumb, perhaps irreversible decision, a care about leaving them all behind. A few bad shroom trips later, she's still the same way.

She tried the meds. So much that she didn't remember trying the meds. Whenever doctors asked, she had to shake her head and pretend it was a long time ago. It finally is. The natural lifestyle was worse, though, probably. The mania kept her alive for the most part, awake and bigger than life. Always buying the best, she was effortlessly good with money and managed to make the financial aid last. She drove her mom's car carelessly and ran into a motorcyclist. He didn't have insurance so she won the case. No one even had to find out she was drunk.

Mel puts out the joint on the lighter itself, purposefully destroying it. Ah, whatever. Fuck Rodrigo. One of the reasons she finds herself so down in the dumps as of late is in part due to him and his using her. Someone who won't let you call them your boyfriend shouldn't get a boyfriend's privileges. Fuck him, and fuck men, and fuck this, fucking lighter's safety band gets jammed anyway.

All her stuff's on the bed. She looks around at the floor and it doesn't get any better. With her glasses dirty, she separates the tasks ahead of her in stacks of mass in the make-believe nets of her mind arranged by time consumption.

Unamused, she begins by putting her clothes away in the closet. She brought her underwear in nice cotton bags, and that's where they stay on a shelf. She stuffs all her T-shirts in one corner and pants in another. In between, to switch it up, she finds her pencil case and tapes a promotional *It's Always Sunny in Philadelphia* poster her mom got her for her birthday. She couldn't bring it rolled, so she had to fold it in fourths, but it doesn't look that bad, the room gradually becoming hers.

Once she's somewhat finished, she crawls in bed with the covers all the way up, closing her eyes and reaching down under. She must focus. Pornography doesn't provide the best orgasms. Quick and hollow, unfulfilling like a man's. Plus the internet can lead to trouble. All kinds of trouble. Not long ago she received an e-mail from the internet company warning her to stop trying to access child porn, which was super weird. Could she have done it and forgotten about it? Days later it came as an epiphany: the Rob Lowe sex tape! She probably didn't classify it as child porn in her head given the whole case, how the sixteen-year-old could legally fuck but not be recorded or something. Basically, my bad. Because Mel had already considered whether she was a pedophile or not. She was confused at times when she thought about little girls. But it wasn't what you might expect. The girls were pubescent, too, just very young. And they were all taken by force. Even if she didn't want to in the beginning, it tended to turn into that. She's guilty of having searched for that too, and the things she saw marked her. There was this one where a man gets raped repeatedly by two dozen inmates in a Brazilian prison. It stole a part of her soul. Did she learn her lesson? It's hard to say. She went through her bestiality phase without thinking much of it, so of course anything below that was fair game. At the end of it all, she was so desensitized she had a hard time finding a healthy fantasy to beat off to. Hating herself for it, she goes for the usual. Just to get her to come, just this one last time. No tween will suffer this anymore, she swears.

Out of control, she jerks up and down and up and down, her eyes open wide staring at the ceiling, the window, slowly the room getting back together, making sense, the song she had stuck in her head, how much money she has in the bank, that thing she can't forget to do, wide awake, put your hand back in its place, everything settled, back on track.

She pretends to be asleep while her mind stays awake. It's a life she's grown accustomed to, but she won't settle for it. What a sad story to waste away the time doing nothing. A dog emits a petty bark. An ambulance roars by. Mel's voice resonating in her head only gets louder, never quieter, building up for the day when she can no longer hear reality, tormented by her irremediable mind.

3

The comforter absorbs the sunlight coming in through the blinds, lulling Mel into the possibility of catching some shuteye until a knock on her door announces: "Let's go, Mel, psychiatrist!" And so she gets out of bed, puts her jeans on, tucks in the pockets, and faces the tired, intolerable Herman. She makes up for it by having forgotten to take her night meds again, her head pulsating and her mood swinging.

But Herman, no, he's always like this early in the day. He drinks coffee but doesn't consider himself a coffee addict. 'Maybe he is, maybe he isn't' is his attitude, so yes, it's likely that he is. Sometimes because it's tradition, sometimes because it's spontaneous. The kind of coffee doesn't matter to him since he delights in trying new flavors. It's truly gratifying when a risk turns out to be delicious. Laura is a little bit more particular about her coffee, but she rarely touches the stuff anyway. She's more likely to open a beer upon arriving home. She takes off her shoes and puts on music. It's so dead without her.

Mel isn't all that worried about Laura. She'll just have to like her one way or the other. The picture of her and Herman in the living room doesn't present her as someone to fear. After figuring out that her dad asked Laura to move in with him but she said no, Mel feels she's got an advantage. She's willing to live with Herman—for the most part—and that woman he's so infatuated with these days isn't. It's gotta count for something.

"You have to tell her everything, Mel. Don't be embarrassed about anything."

"What do I gotta be embarrassed about?" Herman shrugs his shoulders without making eye contact, his hand reaching for the slice of toast with jelly in front of him. "I want some." He points to the cupboard. "Thanks."

"If you want her to help you, you know how it is."

Mel blinks furiously, deciding she doesn't want food actually. She turns around and goes into the bathroom to do her pee, wash face, brush teeth routine. She leaves her hair disheveled, too jittery to take her time with her looks. After all, she's trying to be sincere.

Herman walks way ahead of Mel towards the Malibu and let's it warm up as the young one makes it deliberately along the garage. When she gets in, she turns on the radio and keeps searching for a decent station for a long while on the freeway before giving up. Traffic isn't too bad and they get to the doctor's office before the silence can become alarming. In the waiting room, Herman picks up one of the *Time* magazines while Mel goes on Instagram. Some minutes later, the doctor opens the door.

"Melanie—sorry, Mel...aina Nicchi?" Mel nods with a smile. "Hi, nice to meet you," she says to Mel, giving her her hand to shake.

Herman purses his lips unsure whether his being here is relevant. When Mel was younger, he cared the most about her mental health, seeing what her mother couldn't see. He had a special understanding of their daughter that neither could deny. Mel is, unknown to him, totally aware of their special bond. She calls it: "Bipolar disorder."

Dr. Geyser looks up from underneath her glasses and appears to nod in a zig zag motion, giving her the benefit of the doubt.

"Here, take this," she says to her new case, handing her a copy of a test to help diagnose her. Finding it cheap, Mel takes the piece of paper and reaches into her purse for a pen. "Is that your favorite color?" the doctor asks, keeping Mel from answering the second question.

"What?"

"Your pen. It's purple."

Mel in turn finds it odd and responds, "Not really," because it really is not. That would be teal. She goes on to finish the test and hands it in to the doctor who scans it quickly and makes a mark or two.

"Yes, it seems so. Bipolar disorder."

"Rapid cycling."

"And why do you think you have this? A parent or—"

"Yeah, my father. My father's bipolar."

"Is that the man in the waiting room?" Mel nods. "Is he under medication?" Mel shakes her head. Dr. Geyser angles her neck, her blonde bangs falling on her eyelashes in a playful act. "Does he know he's bipolar?"

"No," Mel says with a bit of a croak like it sometimes happens. "But I'm pretty sure. I mean, he's under other meds, just not the right kind."

"What about your mother?"

"I don't know what her problem is, but it's not this."

"You and your mother fight a lot?"

"Yeah, sometimes."

"And with your father?"

"Mostly he just gets mad at me."

The doctor takes some notes on her pad. Mel pauses, giving her time to write. It's moments like these when she's polite, when it would help her to show her rage.

"How long have you been aware of your condition?"

"Um, I got diagnosed when I was sixteen. They said to wait and see if the depression went away or if it came back."

"Did it come back?"

"It never went away."

"How was your childhood?"

"It sucked." Dr. Geyser makes a crooked half-note. "Parents got divorced when I was little. Same ole tragic story."

"Was your father absent after that?"

"He moved away to remarry. Always too busy to visit."

"So have you tried medication for this before?"

"Yeah, a few times. I got 'em all written down," Mel says, diving into her giant purse to extract a ripped piece of paper from it. "Ativan. Paxil. Celexa. Propranolol. Abilify. And there might be another one. I'm not sure. It's been a while."

"Why did you stop taking them?"

"Well, the Ativan's always just been temporary. Any time I have a bad episode, I get it prescribed. Paxil made me worse. Made me suicidal. Celexa, too. Propranolol, I don't even know what that was for. And the Abilify left me like a fucking zombie. It also made me gain weight. That only depressed me more."

"How long ago was that?"

"Sixteen to eighteen."

"And right now you are..."

"Twenty-one."

"You've been without medication since?"

"Yup. Up until my accident recently."

"What were you up to all that time?"

"College."

"How was that?"

"Didn't work out."

"You said one of the medications made you suicidal?"

"Two. Both Paxil and Celexa. But I get suicidal often. Just at the time it was the first attempts."

"You've had how many?"

"I would say just four real ones."

"When was the last one?"

"About a month ago. No, like six weeks."

"What made you do it?"

"I was feeling stressed. And alone."

"How did you do it?"

"Took a bunch of Vicodin, had a few drinks. Best time of my life."

"Did you plan it ahead of time?"

"Yeah."

"Do you still feel suicidal?"

"Every day."

"Are you thinking of attempting it again?"

"No, never. I always find this relief in waking up alive so...not for me."

Dr. Geyser uncrosses her legs and looks at Mel straight in the eye. Mel tends to have this effect on doctors. Other patients must be awful. They're probably in denial, ignorant, closed-minded to learning how to deal with things that are probably never gonna go away. That must be why when Mel shows up with this 'here's the deal' attitude, they give her some admiration with a hint of pity, because as educated as she is on the subject, she still suffers from it.

As it can never be avoided, Dr. Geyser goes on to ask about sex and drugs as usual. Mel does her best to not hold back, but she methodically colors over it, either softening or hardening the facts. It's her story in her own words.

The consultation lasts sixteen minutes, one more than it tends to take with psychiatrists. The doctor recommends she continue the treatment she's on—a mood stabilizer, an anti-depressant, and an anxiolytic—and advices Mel to start exercising. After everything she heard in her office, Dr. Geyser gives Herman a nod, which he takes as a friendly goodbye, standing up and opening the door, exiting before Mel.

"What did she give you?" he asks in the car on their way to CVS.

"She just increased the dosage of what they gave me in Riverside. Lamictal and Wellbutrin and...what's it called? I forget the name of the other one."

"Three?!"

"Yeah, they're supposed to work together."

"And how much are they?"

"I don't fucking know!"

Herman bites his finger before switching lanes. With his daughter, it costs a lot every time. Either her health or her interests, the broken bones, the hard covers, all very high-maintenance.

They get to the pharmacy and wait around as the order gets processed. Herman ends up paying something like forty-five bucks, frowning as he swipes the card, Mel nearing tears, suddenly hurt by this. She hides it well, and they get back to the car for another few blocks until they reach the apartment building, Herman stopping right by the stairs that lead to their home.

"Finish unpacking," he says just as she bangs the car door shut.

The car makes a tight U-turn and leaves for Herman's job in the San Fernando Valley. It would be smarter if he lived there—it's cheaper and closer to everything—but after meeting Laura through his parents' friends, he sticks around her in Agoura Hills. She must have a dear grip on him. But Laura is his Rodrigo: barely responsive in comparison to their passion. Even though they're worlds apart in experience, Mel is pretty sure she understands.

Lungs deflated by the stairs, Mel passes the first apartment with expectancy. Chipper and valiant suddenly, her guts fry and the smoke rises through her esophagus, leaving a disgusting taste in her mouth. But every interesting thing that ever happens is accompanied by stomach acid. Mel slows down, stopping to turn back on her heels as soon as she hears the television on. Sounds like a reality show. Upon further inspection, she sees the light is on, and as unnecessary as that seems at this time of day, it's a good sign. Full of hope like she's never believed in anything before, her irrationality proves beneficial when she doesn't stop to think about it and knocks on the door two times, then another to make it sound better. The movement inside subsides, or tries to, then quickly ends up by the door. Mel smiles without looking into the peephole.

"Yeah?"

The door flings open and as soon as it stays put, Mel has to swallow some vomit down. A stick-thin peroxide blonde in a red silk robe with makeup smeared all over her face observes Mel before exhaling cigarette smoke. She moves a ruby pendant hanging from a white gold chain around her neck compulsively as if caught at a bad time. For a quick moment, Mel thinks she sees stars, panicking she's about to start running given the amount of adrenaline she's just spurted. The physical ailment she notices before she can start to understand why. Mh, this isn't Jameson. The pendant goes from side to side, leaving her in a perpetual feeling of déjà vu. She takes a deep breath and looks at the girl's face with the confidence of already knowing a person, her stomach growling as if telling her this is not someone she wants to know, really. Confused, she maintains eye contact. The girl's overdrawn eyebrows look off, the right one permanently arched higher than the left, it seems, or maybe she's truly unimpressed by anything while deadly curious at the same time. The more they stay this way, the more the symptoms continue. Her head feels like it just got kicked around a group of kids, and it shoots pain all along her body as if she were covered in bruises. This must be Artie.

"Sorry," Mel blurts out as soon as she can. "Jameson. I was looking for Jameson."

"He's asleep," she answers, trying to keep her from seeing whatever's going on inside by blocking the doorway with a wide stance, her cleavage becoming more and more exposed as she tightens the hold on her waist. With dead cold eyes, she pretends to be weirded out by Mel's reaction. "Why? What do you need?"

"I just thought maybe he was free," Mel manages to articulate as she pants. "Just tell him I stopped by."

"And who are you?"

"The new neighbor," she answers.

"Okay," Artie says sluggishly. "I'll tell him the new neighbor stopped by."

There is great disdain in her tone, but Mel feels bad for how uncouth she was. It could have been easier if she hadn't been caught off guard like that. With nothing left to say, Mel takes a step back. At the same time, Artie begins to close the door.

"No, wait!" says a voice from inside, a second before Jameson appears putting on a stained white T-shirt, mismatched socks shuffling into hand-me-down slippers, his eyes puffy and red. "I'm awake."

Artie pulls the door open all the way in surprise, revealing a fully dressed man curled up on the couch and breakfast food sizzling on a pan. Jameson moves in short steps trying to look as presentable as possible, mindful that he looks like shit.

"You're up this early?" Artie asks, taking a wisp off her strawberry Kiss Superslim. She never went to bed. As for Jameson, he laid in his. "You okay?"

"Couldn't sleep."

"We have things in common," Mel jumps in, her right foot on the threshold. She regrets saying so by bowing her head. "What's up?"

"Nothing, 'sup with you?" he asks, first amiably, then concerned. "And no smoking indoors, Artie. Seriously!"

He insists on stepping closer to Mel, also trying to cover up what's going on. By now, Artie has made it back to the kitchen to flip whatever she's cooking.

"Wanna come hang out?" she asks, sensing his apartment out of bounds. "My dad's gone—"

"Sure," he responds, closing the door behind him. He opens it again and grabs his keys from a hook on the wall, yelling: "Be back later!" The sleeping man moves, his legs rubbing against the denim of his jeans. "Don't worry, I got the stuff in my pocket."

It makes her look. She sees the bulge of a canister. He makes a face as if to indicate how rude of her it was to look. It makes her titter a bit, her almost-freakout almost forgotten en route to getting high with the closest thing she has to a friend.

In her room, Jameson goes for the crate of records instantly, his opinion on each one ready. "This is the sound of America," or, "People forget what an incredible voice he has," and of course, "I never really got into them."

"You should help me set it up," she says, pointing at Grandpa's gift on the floor, confident she might get what she wants.

He eyes the stereo and nods, then proceeds to take out the marijuana accompanied by a miniature metal pipe. Poised, he packs a bowl, tiny bits falling on Mel's carpet. She thinks she'll remember where they end up so she can get to them later, but she won't.

"Your roommate," she mentions as soon as she catches her breath, not sure what she's trying to tell him. What just happened anyway? Did her blood pressure go down? When she closed her eyes she saw silhouettes, salivating the flavor of blood, her ears muffled as if time had stopped. Really intense. "It's like I've seen her in a dream or something."

Jameson looks up thinking. Artie looks like all those basic bitches: rich, tan, bulimic. Her breasts aren't all that large, but they're definitely fake. If it's gotta be something, then it's gotta be that.

"Scrawny white girls, what can I say?" She waits for him to give it more thought, and he reconsiders. "Actually, no, you're right," he praises at her blank stare. "She says she had a line in a movie once. She won't tell me which, though. Looked for her on IMDb. Nothing. Must have used a different name." Mel looks out the window. "She's got a great voice." He appears to be losing her. "So you said you couldn't sleep either?"

"It takes time to adjust to a new place. But, I mean, I don't sleep much anywhere anyway," she responds, working hard to keep in mind what's currently going on.

"I used to have pretty bad insomnia," he shares, taking greens.

"When I'm feeling blue, I sleep all day. So it all depends on my mood."

"Yeah, now I usually oversleep. I love it." He passes the pipe. "That's why 'I'm Only Sleeping' is my new favorite song."

"*Revolver* happens to be my favorite Beatles album."

"I feel like I could have guessed that about you," he says, standing up. "Let's set this up then."

"What's your favorite?"

Checking the cables coming from the back, Jameson clenches his jaw.

"I'm not sure. It could be *Rubber Soul. Abbey Road.* It might even be *Revolver.* They're all my favorites. Even The White Album, half of it is horrid, but the other half is brilliant. *Help!* That was their first serious stuff, that's when shit got real. And, come on, what about early Beatles, what about the B-sides? Although, I mean, *Sgt. Pepper's.*"

"I feel you," she sympathizes. "Mine changes. Like my favorite Beatle changes."

"Same. Right now I'm with Paul."

"Right?!" she asks enthusiastically, perhaps too much.

He keeps working on the stereo. "I was always a big Lennon fan, and I always will be, but I'm going through a McCartney phase, I dunno. Where do you want the speakers, by the way?"

"I've no idea. I guess one over there," she says, her palm extended at the corner facing the bed. "And the other, like, right there."

"Okay, so let's move it," Jameson mumbles, blocking her from accessing any of the equipment so she may not lift a finger. Just trying to be a gentleman. "I mostly became disillusioned with Lennon as a person."

"He was kind of a piece of shit."

"Totally bipolar."

"But, see, at the same time, my favorite songs are George's. I like how he feels more."

"He was more of a big picture kind of guy. Still a douchebag. Do you have an extension chord?" Mel shakes her head,f let down. "Well," he clears his throat, "I have one you can borrow, if you want."

"Sure."

He goes for the door with a quick: "Be right back."

Not in a hurry, he crosses Herman's living room and goes outside. His breathing is hard, his breath horrible. When he gets to his apartment, he's gonna do mouthwash. For a second he forgets what he's coming here for, unlocking the door only once, as Artie locks it. Pollo is still passed out on the couch. It grosses the shit out of Jameson, this behavior. Artie eats a scrambled egg bagel sandwich standing up by the sink, an open can of Diet Coke at arm's reach. The robe will disrobe at any second. She must be strung out. Another paltry little existence of self-abuse. All of them. The whole lot of them.

"Who was that?" she asks, food falling out of her mouth and into—well, good thinking, Artie—the sink.

"Uh, she just moved."

Jameson goes into his room and opens his closet. He looks in a basket of cables until he finds an extension chord that's long enough, turning around to go to the bathroom only he finds Artie standing there silently by his door.

"What's her name?" she asks sternly with that ability of hers to look at someone straight in the eye until they give. "Who is she?"

"Melanie or something."

He tries going around her but she follows backwards.

"Melanie?"

"Yup."

"She's weird."

Satisfied but angry, for some reason, she retreats into the kitchen as if her uneasy behavior made her pretty. He used to think she was cool, they were friends, their music was bomb. And then they moved in together. The music stopped happening, the friendship died, and she became the worst human being he's ever met. No way around it.

As he hurries out, Artie throws the roll of paper towels at her brother with a loud: "Get the fuck up!" She seems to be up to the task of having someone to gossip with. She'll probably talk shit on Mel. And Jameson, of course. That's a given.

He's happy to make it to Mel's until he knocks on her door and hears her having a conversation. She lets him in and lifts a finger to indicate a minute. Jameson goes on to use the extension chord.

"Okay, he's back. I gotta go," she says, holding her cell phone lazily to her neck. "Bye." She hangs up, throws the phone on the bed, and looks at what Jameson is doing. "Do you have a car?" she asks him.

"Yeah. Why? You wanna get food?"

"Kinda."

"You like sandwiches? There's a Togo's nearby."

"You know, I've always said it 'to gos,' not 'toe goes,' I don't know why."

"So you do wanna go."

"Yeah, yeah."

"Lemme just finish this…"

Mel steps back and sits on the bed. Waiting gives her time to contemplate the last…half hour? Fifteen minutes? She isn't sure. It isn't just the weed, it's her panic attack. Moments of distress sometimes get difficult to recall fully or correctly. Certain things slow down, others speed up, the volume silences, the race in her mind gets louder, and then it pops in sound, somewhat back to normal. She imagines that's what it's like to deal with guns.

"'Kay, this should work," Jameson says softly.

She hands him *Ram* and he puts it on, placing the needle carefully on the slightly warped disc. "Too Many People" starts playing, popping once, twice, and then it seems to settle down.

"This is love," Jameson says a ways into it.

"It's beautiful." Jameson nods and his throat gargles loudly. Mel laughs at this in a sympathetic manner, but perhaps it doesn't come off exactly as meant. "Happens to me all the time," she says to make sure she's not being misunderstood. "During tests, especially. My throat or my stomach will just blergggh for everyone to hear. It's distracting. There's just too much acid in there."

"Yeah, you get bad heartburn?"

"Sometimes. Now it's mostly gastritis."

"Is that like a baby ulcer?"

"Pretty accurate way of putting it."

"Let's get sandwiches then. Coat them stummies."

She gets up first, he last, somewhat lingering to appreciate the look of her while she opens an Altoids tin, offering him one. He takes two, lowering his gaze when she looks at him. She's wearing a wide Indian dress with large pockets, the design in shades of beige. It hangs weightlessly off her slumped shoulders. Through the holes of her Converse, he sees her neon pink socks. At this point, the shoes are merely a formality. She faintly skips in them on their way out, playing with the possibility of them falling apart at any second.

"'Cause there's the Jews you know. And then there's The Jews, you know?"

It's a good joke. Even she, when notified of its brilliance, agrees that yeah, maybe it's funny. She was looking away holding on to her sandwich. Her brown eyes, though not big all the time, are big when she speaks, but mostly she keeps quiet. She listens. He finds her earnestly interested in what he has to say, and he has a lot to say. Except she doesn't get much of his jokes. Or maybe she does and just doesn't deem them worthy of laughter. An air of mystery fills her dark stare. Must be a secret, he thinks. She must have a secret she needs to get out.

He could be someone to confide in. After all the things they have in common, they could only understand one another.

But going past every detail of similarity or agreeableness— how her hair has a hue of honey in the sunlight, her tendency to unconsciously drum with her hands on the closest surface during moments of no conversation, her dismissal of anything she doesn't know about, secretly keeping a list to study— though it's kind of curious, she asks about Artie in a different manner than she asks whether he's seen *Oddsac* or been attacked by a stray dog.

"Artie what?"

"Artemis Waltz," he tells her. "Met her in Simi Valley. Punk crowd. She seemed out of place, so I started talking to her. As soon as I told her I was a musician, she got really excited 'cause she was trying to put a band together. So then like that that same week we got together with my friend Pete on drums and just started writing. We all had stuff we were working on, and we ended up recording our EP in the following months. Then Pete fucked my girlfriend, so he got kicked out. And now it's been six months since Artie and I rehearse or work on anything. She's always fucking mad at me or 'feeling sick' or just gone. There is no band anymore."

"No more Night Mara?"

"I'm afraid not."

"I'm sorry about Pete," she says with a warm look.

"It was only a three-month-long affair I had to discover after arduous work. I nearly went insane."

"Fuuuck, man. That sucks."

Neither of them can say much after that. They finish their sandwiches, and he asks if she wouldn't mind accompanying him to Ross, somehow segueing into the Iraq War, getting talking about other stuff. He might have said too much too quickly. When he drops her off at her doorstep, she's distant.

Mel doesn't appear to be a fake person. She can't mask her emotions. Or maybe he's simply super skilled at reading her.

"'Cause there's the Jews you know. And then there's The Jews, you know?" Jameson replays it in his head during his shift, giving him a distracted look that doesn't help with the tips. His sleeplessness is rather conspicuous too. Thankfully it's a slow night.

On the way back home, his intestines start hurting and he does what he can to get there faster, the old Chevy Cavalier not making it past fifty. When he can't hold it in any longer, that's when he parks and runs to the bathroom, not acknowledging Artie on his way in. He sprays lavender air freshener and lights a match, and when he steps out, Artie gives him a pissed off look, saying something about the rent, then gives him two capsules of molly in exchange for the Xanax she knows he bought from their friend Cassie a couple of days ago. He had his suspicions that Cassie wasn't selling to Artie anymore—who knows what Artie must have done to piss her off—but Artie would find a way to get it anyway, and his giving it to her is the safest method. He can get more Xanax form Cassie any time.

After a sad dinner, Jameson cheers himself up with one of the few pleasures of this world: taking a long, hot shower. Screw anyone with their 'save water' bullshit. Yeah, there's a drought, the whole world is fucked. Like his showers are the problem. Blame him, though, sure, why not? Tell him to be mindful of his water usage when the mere concept of golf courses is just—it's just wrong, man.

He plays guitar for an hour or so. A lot of ideas flood him musically. He executes what he can before twisting his back, bones cracking, to look out the window, mulling over the day. Mel, a few apartments away, could be up to anything. The last time he saw her was twelve hours ago. He must really like her, feeling pulled by a new hole in which to miss her. Just as long as it's reciprocated, he concludes softly.

"You're friend-zoning me," he said when she refused to let him pay for her sandwich. She was like, don't even. "I'm just kidding," he had to add.

Jameson pisses one last time, remembers to take his meds—unlike every other day—and lays in bed for ten minutes, thinking about the same things.

"'Cause there's the Jews you know. And then there's The Jews, you know?"

The Quetiapine does its thing and he falls asleep on his back. As he thought he would, he dreams about Mel, the only pure thing in his quotidian nightmares.

4

Jameson gets up just as tired as he was when he went to bed. It's about one in the afternoon and Artie's gone. A note on the fridge reads: *Leave rent on table. Pollo will get and bring to Palm Springs.* The redaction repulses Jameson. Also because Pollo shouldn't come and go as he pleases just because he's got the spare key. He looks past it and retrieves a box of mini pancakes from the freezer. He makes himself hungry with a bowl and abates the rumbling in his stomach with a light breakfast.

Without debating the issue much—he slept on it, woke up feeling the same—he takes out his cell phone and texts Mel to see what she's up to today, it being his day off.

It causes Mel's pocket to buzz, but she doesn't hear it. She's walking up the road, her armpits wet in the discretion of a black Tyrone Biggums T-shirt. Some time after Herman left for work this morning, she made herself get up from her taxing wakefulness and took her meds. Soon after, she couldn't ignore the energy she felt, and so she got dressed, laced up her shoes, and left on a walk that still keeps her occupied many hours later. Her mouth is dry, her forehead burning, and she must have a blister or two. What's best is she doesn't feel any of these things, the sudden burst of life powering her numb. Must be the 100 mg Wellbutrin—if the 50 mg ones got her out of bed, who knows how far these will take her.

She ignores Rodrigo's text about his getting drunk with their friends, not at all interesting, and then is reminded by her mother about the gym she's supposed to join. But by now Mel has totally gone past that. Like, sure, it was a good idea. It still is. Now is it realistic? Is it worth it? Because when you get to these questions, that's when it becomes obvious that no, it's not. It's all just shit to fill up your empty life with. You think you have a purpose? What does it even matter? Even if you make it, you won't make it out alive. Everybody dies. So fuck going to the gym. That shit's depressing.

"Hi. What?" she answers into her cell phone, irritated by the interruption. She was just about to enter a movie theater that's hiring.

"Hey, just—just wondering how you were," Rodrigo responds, sounding sorry to have made the call as if even his better judgment knew it was wrong to do so.

"All right. Walking around applying for jobs."

"Cool."

"Cool."

"I'm helping my sister move a couch later. What—what are you up to?"

"Walking around applying for jobs."

"Right."

"Yeah," she sighs.

"Well, I guess I'll talk to you later."

"'Kay, bye."

He stays on the line without saying anything until she decides to hang up. There goes that.

The human resources lady hands Mel an application to fill out on the spot. Using her purple pen, she ponders on her personal information, education, and work experience, each section with less and less writing in that order. She hands it to the all-business-like lady with a gentle, close-mouthed smile and returns to the humidity outside. Hopefully it rains again. We need it to.

The walk back sounded like it should be easier, going down the slopes of Thousand Oaks, but it ends up being more exhausting than going up. When she nears her street, her cell phone vibrates, the synthesizer grooving, and she looks for it in her giant purse full of crap for a good thirty seconds before she can answer.

"Hi, this is Stephanie from Cinerama. I wanted to set up an interview with you..."

Nailed it.

Peeled back to white, there isn't anything Mel can't have. After all this time, all these chances. No one would let her get lost in a half-way-there life, no matter how hard she tried. Strong arms would linger by the edge to save her.

Skinny-ass Rodrigo texts again. She doesn't check it until she goes up the slope of the building complex entrance. *sorry if i sounded weird. i'm super baked.* What his deal is lately, Mel doesn't know, but that's because she doesn't know how much he knows about her 'accident.' He used to take days to respond to her texts, manipulating her emotions with a puppeteer's ease. Now that he's pulling harder, Mel sees how the strings are about to sever.

Eventually she reads Jameson's text, her urge to delay it part of her self-destructive behavior. *are you up to anything today? it's my day off and i'm gonna buy weed.* Though she's tired, her legs incapable of any more movement, her clothes drenched, her face red, she kind of, yeah, she's down. The more she thinks about it, the more she's gonna change her mind. She'll keep coming up with excuses to stay put, punishing herself for something.

can you get me some? that way there's more to smoke.
i'm in the valley right now. how much do you want?
30 dollars worth.

Idly, Mel goes to the living room, swings about, and sits on the sofa. She turns on the TV and tries to find something to watch. Unlike her mother's house where she has a whole collage of family pictures in silver frames on the entertainment center, there are no distracting objects around the tube here. In fact, there is barely any decoration at all. Very Herman-like, she decrees, because what's the use of buying something that doesn't do anything? Money that just sits there. The only thing there is is a picture of him and Laura in a restaurant celebrating their one year anniversary. You can tell her theory is correct once more given the free nature of these kinds of photos.

The more she stares at it with the TV blurring in the corner of her eye, the more she begins to feel things. She looks around before getting up to investigate. The thought of going into her dad's bedroom hadn't occurred to her yet—she hadn't needed anything—so she doesn't know what to expect. Upon inching through the open door, first her nose, her right heel last, she comes in contact with a clean room bordering on the bare. He's got a baby cactus by the window. How personal. Anger fuels the tears in her eyes going back to the refrigerator: a Las Vegas magnet holding Subway coupons. There is nothing, absolutely nothing that recognizes her existence in the world.

Could it be to appear more available to women, or because if she didn't give him anything to put up, he wouldn't think to do so himself? Those are her more optimistic options to go with. It wouldn't make sense to demean herself by taking personal offense. Her blood still feels hot, but her head grows more stable with its decision to let it go. She makes sure to savor the rare feeling.

She jumps in the shower and beatboxes until she hears the front door opening and closing. A faint conversation is being carried out. Mel's unsure if she locked the bathroom door, so she hurries up.

"Lettie got so drunk, she was trying to get with this young bartender."

"And I bet she did, too."

Mel gets out to lock the door before it's too late. She dries up and regrets not having brought her clothes in with her. It's pretty early in the day, but she doesn't know her dad's schedule yet. She does everything she has to do in the bathroom in one take and finally comes out to the living room.

Though she could have walked right past them into her room safely without manners, Mel freezes, holding on to her towel before both Herman and Laura, presumably.

"Hi."

"Nice to meet you, Melaina," goes Laura, taking a step forward, causing Mel to retreat.

"Sorry, I'll just go get dressed first," she finally lets out in an awkward, rather mean tone before mumbling to herself as she turns her back on them.

"I'll ask her if she wants to go to my parents' for dinner," Herman says. "I need to give my mom some stuff she asked me to print out."

He hands Laura a beer and makes himself a coffee. She keeps telling him about her trip to Las Vegas for a friend's bachelorette party. It's the third time this year.

Mel introduces herself to Laura very carelessly. She hasn't got her glasses on, she doesn't hug, she should have at least attempted to cover up the dark circles under her eyes, and what's most annoying is her callous behavior. When he looks at her, Herman sees someone who doesn't give a fuck if today is the end of the world. Laura tries to get something out of Mel, but her lines don't deliver. It's as if Mel never outgrew adolescence. What she doesn't know is Mel is playing her and her dad. Mel isn't quite sure how, but she's playing them. She makes it obvious when she excuses herself not ten minutes into it to go shut herself in her room.

Tired of waiting for Jameson, she picks at the skin on her neck and checks her phone every couple of minutes. He better get home before she leaves for her grandparents' house where she will be welcomed with all sorts of delicious food and drink, or it'll go to waste.

Instagram keeps her distracted for the thirty or so minutes it takes for her phone to display a happy *i'm back. wanna come over?* She might have never been so excited in her life. Grabbing her wallet, she bustles past the adults saying she'll be back soon, and when she gets there, she goes for three knocks, only the door opens in two.

"It's not that I'm scared of death, like, how sad. No, no. I'm sure death is fine. I'm not affected by my unconsciousness when I'm unconscious. But when I think about it—and it's gonna happen right now, it does every time—I just think about it and then this feeling of dread runs through me like a poison. My vision darkens all around and I can't breathe. I have to take a deep breath and shake it off otherwise it consumes me."

"Claustrophobia," Jameson says.

"Yeah."

He rolls another joint, she sips water. They've been talking and toking for the last two hours. He tried playing guitar, but she didn't care for it, leaving her uninvolved and all, though she did applaud after his performance of "A Day in the Life," sharing with him what she called her only talent: clasping her hands behind her back and twisting her arms askew until she brought them to the front over her head without letting go, then stepping over the hoop bringing them back to the start, telling him to not get any ideas about her double-jointedness. Now they just keep talking and toking, toking and talking, and he can't decide if she's opening up because she likes him or because she's not trying to impress him. He needs to ask her without doing so.

"It's nice having you around."

Mel grins, her eyes two small red dots. He watched her hair dry in the heat. All the clouds are gone, hopefully taking that rain where it's most needed. Back to the warm, dusty air of Ventura County. Although, as Jameson pointed out to Mel a few minutes earlier, their part of Agoura Hills is in L.A. County. Made no sense to them either.

"I was afraid I wasn't gonna make any friends, but this has been so easy."

"I'm glad you asked me for pot."

"I'm glad you helped me with my records."

"I'm glad I was here smoking pot."

They contemplate on that for a second. It's so calm yet lively being together.

The moment she leaves some time later to go to her grandparents' house, everything else that isn't Mel comes back to him. She said she'd free up at night and they could watch a movie maybe. This might be it.

He runs to his laptop and checks his options. Had he mentioned any movies she hadn't seen? He can't remember. Even though his collection is solid, he steals a few more, whatever just leaked.

It takes him a while to tidy up his room. He's grateful for Mel's insistence earlier that they remain on the balcony and not go inside. If he'd remembered how dirty it was in here, he wouldn't have invited her.

Jameson rids himself of dead skin with a pink scrubby from the dollar store. He gets his face, arms, torso, back, legs, feet. Then he washes his junk, but upon inspection, he decides it doesn't look that great. He gets out, dripping so heavily the rug soaks, and opens a drawer to obtain a pair of scissors. With as much precision as he is capable of, he trims his pubes a bit, making sure not to go too far. It's not that he thinks he can fuck her, it's that he's gotta be ready just in case.

Eight miles away, Mel's caught on to that too. And she likes Jameson, in fact, he's awesome, but then there's Rodrigo, like, not that far away in case they ever see each other. They can't, anyway. They don't have cars. They won't. But even if they did, she isn't feeling it. She may have been close to being obsessed with him—you don't know how tall girls need tall boys—if it weren't for the fact that she thinks the worst of him. You could say their relationship is complicated, to put it mildly. If it were up to Mel, she'd describe it as emotional abuse. Rodrigo calls it 'hanging out.'

But the problem isn't Rodrigo per se. The problem is what causes problems with Rodrigo, any boyfriend, any boy, any friend, anyone, and that is her. When her bipolar states had phases months long, everything was sort of, eh, all right. She'd shift to one pole and remain there for a while, so that while things were still chaotic, there remained some consistency. Manic, depressive, manic, depressive. But now that she's cycling so rapidly, sometimes several, several times a day, it's nearly impossible to stand her. She gives herself pep talks any chance she finds positivity, but she shouldn't hold her breath on that.

Grandma slowly gets up from her chair and starts making it to her bedroom to lie down. She's full of pains all the time, especially when she's grown bored of her guests. To Mel it may be that Laura isn't well liked. Grandpa watches the news with a glass of wine.

"Goddamn ISIS," he mutters into the drink. "Fucking Muslims."

"Throw a bomb and start over, right?" Mel says to him, catching him by surprise.

"That's right," he scoffs in return, his grey mustache rustling with his stale breath.

Herman looks at Mel like what the fuck? But Mel doesn't buy into his liberal bullshit.

"I meant for the whole human race," she says in her defense.

She looks at Laura and sees the same concern in her brow. Hey, at least they have things in common. Yet Mel can tell she's not like the women that came before her. She's another gem in Herman's collection. His ex-wife was one of those hippie broads why with her beads, yoga and big afro. She lit incense and Herman had to get used to it, asthma and all. And before that was Mel's mother, a no-nonsense, hardworking foreign woman. Now there's this Laura person, teaching philosophy at a private high school with a Rogue hair job and huge tits. This last fact is only mentioned out of obligation to their tremendous, distracting, somewhat belittling size. It's hard to take her seriously when those big knockers simply can't be hidden. What a nuisance. A burden. Mel laughs to herself. They all expect an explanation but it never comes.

"Go make Grandma some company," Herman orders, embarrassed.

Mel rolls her eyes and does as she's told, going down the paneled hallway past two dozen framed sketches, all done by

Grandma during her pregnancies. Apparently all the hormones inspired her to draw even though she had never showed any interest in the craft before. Once Wesley, Herman's younger brother, was born, she returned to shopping and tennis, abandoning her drawings of birds and fruits and flowers forever. Thus they rest on the wall as a reminder that you never know how your own body's gotta hit ya.

The bedroom is floral. Every bed sheet, curtain, and wall-paper: floral. It looks as such because Grandma does whatever the hell she wants, and sometimes that's not that great. The bedroom is the worst since Grandma and Grandpa don't sleep together. He snores, supposedly. The truth is, they should have divorced who knows how many years ago now had that been popular back then. As a teenager, Herman followed his mother when she went out—maybe he already had his suspicions, maybe not—and saw her getting into another man's car. This he never told his father, but he told his daughter in confidence when she was a kid. Whatever he was trying to get across went over Mel's head. The only thing she remembers besides the story is his regret.

"Hi, Grandma," she says slowly. "You asleep?"

"No, no. Come in." Mel takes a seat on the bed next to her. "Can you pass me the water, love?"

Mel finds the glass she's referring to on the bedside table next to a bunch of pill bottles and a paperback. She hands it to her and notices how wrinkled her grandma's hands are in comparison to her face and neck, shining smoothly under a handful of lifts. She doesn't look too different from the wedding portrait hanging above the vanity table. Mel finds it funny that it's just a picture of the bride, no groom.

"Do you have any pictures of me and Dad? I wanna get one framed so he can put it in his apartment."

"Ohh," says Grandma Lisa high pitched. "Do I have any pictures. Please." She sits up but stops before moving her legs. It must be her hip. "Ow."

"Where are they?"

"They're right there in the closet," she says, pointing at the farthest corner. "In a black shoe box on the floor." Mel gets on her knees and pulls out said box from behind a row of fancy sandals and pumps. "That box is actually your dad's. He left it here when he moved out of Carine's, and he still hasn't taken it. He took his tapes, I think, but never the pictures. It's on the back of my mind every time he comes over, but I keep forgetting to tell him, so thank goodness you asked."

The kid brings the box over and Grandma Lisa undoes the rubber band around it, lifting the lid. There's not that many pictures in here, but more than half of them are of Mel and Herman.

"I remember him asking my mom for the pictures of us together when they got divorced."

Grandma Lisa nods, picking out a handful to look at. Mel does the same, the nostalgia kicking in. Before the divorce, everything was perfect. Mom and Dad and Mel were best friends. Vacations, made-up games, photo shoots, karaoke, bike rides. Curse the day they called her to the living room saying they had something to tell her. She sat between them on the couch and they both contributed with some kind of physical contact. Like that made it any easier. "We're not in love anymore," they said. So what? Mel should have asked. What about her? She understood family in the sense that they had gotten together to have her, and that bond couldn't be undone. All the sacrifices necessary would have to be made for the child. Otherwise, why have her? Why did she even exist? For the first time, Mel experienced the desire to cease being. The years that followed revealed to Mel that she had never been enough. She learned that her father left her mother when she told him she was pregnant, returning for the latter part of the pregnancy, staying for a good phase that lasted six years. Discontent caught up with him by the time he neared forty, and he freaked out on his life, destroying everything that couldn't be glued back together with the sincerest of apologies, not that he ever tried that approach anyhow. Yet in the last few years, Mel came to see just how similar they are, and that made her give him another chance. Last one for reals this time.

"You know," Mel starts, holding back tears, "Dad taught me to cry. Once we were on a bike ride with my mom and I fell since I had just learned how to ride. I scraped my knee, and it really hurt, and I made sure there was no one else around before allowing myself to cry. And Dad called me out on it, he was like, why do you gotta make sure there's no one else around before allowing yourself to cry? And I realized that, yeah, it was stupid to be ashamed. I had all the right to cry. I shouldn't be judged for it—"

"Your dad's always been a crybaby," Grandma Lisa interrupts.

A bit offended, Mel sets down the pictures she's just looked at and dives for some more.

"When was this?" Mel holds up a picture of Herman grilling burgers and a miserable Mel opening a present in a nice backyard, the balloons matching the flowers. She's about eight and is wearing an extra small adult men's Gorillaz T-shirt. "Or maybe you weren't there."

"No, yes, yes, I was. That was when we stayed at Carine's for a couple of weeks."

"I don't think I ever stayed at Carine's old house. I only went to the other place that wasn't as close to the beach."

And yet here's a picture of the huge house Carine kept for some time after separating from her fancy furniture store-owning first husband. Dread surrounds Mel, and she shakes it off with a deep breath.

"Mel, are you okay?"

"Yeah, just...dizzy. Low blood pressure thing."

"You're so lucky to have low blood pressure. Mine's high and, oh, is it dangerous."

Setting the photo aside, Mel keeps looking at her baby self, kid self, and some loose teenage ones that seem out of place. This father got to see his daughter for a little while a few times a year, sometimes every couple of them, missing out on all the things that mattered, more and more with time, what with school and work and excuses. His memories of her had to be askew. Like for example, the year she spontaneously dyed her hair black at age twelve, right about the same time she wrote that love letter to Warren Foster. Her dad's family were all very supportive and gave her the prettiest of compliments. Mel felt so badass. Then came the fall and she went to school where everyone made fun of her, calling her a goth. Those idiots didn't even know what goth was. She was clearly punk rock. I mean, she brought skinny jeans back. She picked out a pair of jeans at the Goodwill, had her mom sew them tight, and then she added, like, an Adicts patch and safety pins, black studded belt and everything. A year later, everyone was wearing them.

Flipping through them quickly, Mel thinks she's seen at least one picture from every roll of film. This is the time she's ever spent with her father. Quite insignificant. But how must Herman feel, being a parent only sometimes? Distraught or relieved, Mel doesn't really know. She's never asked.

Her fingers go through more pictures until they come into contact with thicker material that doesn't fit in with the rest. Mel pulls out the Polaroid from a mountain of glossy paper without understanding much. It takes her a second to process the image, her respiratory system shutting down for one, two, three seconds...it's her with a friend—it seems—at either side, a boy and a girl. The boy is tall and extremely muscular. The girl is short and chubby. They both have long, light brown hair, trying to force a resemblance between them. She collects hers in a sturdy ponytail, the waves falling fully over her shoulders. He's got his T-shirt on inside out and backwards, the mom-written name *SAMUEL B.* underneath the collar in blue marker.

"Sam," Mel gives out under her breath. Grandma Lisa tries to keep up, her granddaughter suddenly shaking, her eyes coming in and out of focus staring at the Polaroid. "Sam," she says again. "Tilly and Sam."

"Melaina?"

"Sorry," she sniffs. "Can I take this?"

"Take the whole box!"

"Thanks."

Mel leaves to go to the bathroom, the Polaroid crumpled in her back pocket. She pees a little bit before washing her hands and face, then takes out the photo to stare at it some more. They're all distracted, Tilly looking sideways, Sam looking down, Mel right into the camera. The backyard is the same as that picture of Herman grilling and her opening a present. Carine's old house. From the start, she distinguished the place, but the recollection is faint. In fact, it is somewhat blank. The place is there, but there are no emotions attached to it.

"Mel!" A knock on the door. "We're leaving."

"'Kay," she yells, snapping out of it.

During the car ride, Mel tries to get her dad's attention by going through the box of pictures in the backseat, bringing up past memories just to be cut off each time by Laura's retelling of another one of her lame friends' Vegas shenanigans. Mel daydreams until Laura gets dropped off. She holds the car door open, waiting for Mel to switch to the front seat, but it never happens. Laura closes the door and waves goodbye at Mel in the back. It's one of those waves directed at children.

When they get home, Herman yawns once and heads to his room. Wired, Mel leaves the box on the table and locks herself in, sitting on her bed to look at the Polaroid better. The more she examines it, the more she'll find out. But it says nothing. It's just a wrinkled old picture.

She smokes a bowl using the miniature pipe Jameson brought over, doing what she can to level her head. She's been here before, in the uncertainty of blindness, incapable of telling what's what. It stabs you out of nowhere and spins you round the knife.

In attempts to distract herself, she texts Jameson to see if he wants to hang out.

He's has been waiting all day. It gave him time to leave everything ready. Tonight's the night. What that means exactly is debatable. Something, however, has got to happen. He thinks that even if he gets bad vibes, he's gonna tell her...again, something.

He rotates on his axis. With more nervousness than he should allow himself to feel, he feels the feeling once more, that feeling of wanting someone so bad that you can't finish a sentence. Scorned, he thought he'd never love again. Even twenty-four is too young to say never, but he suffered so much it rang true. For a while he gave up, then he didn't wanna be alone, gave it some half-assed tries, and then, now, this.

Mel leaves Rodrigo, or whoever, at the door before embarking on the twenty strides it takes her to get to Jameson's place, and, taking everything into consideration, knocks three times, ready for whatever, unsure of what she wants, constantly denying herself happiness by chasing imitations of it.

Saying the least, Jameson opens the door and lets her in. The place smells like lavender, her favorite. All the lights are off, signaling her to follow him into the bedroom. He leaves the door open as she stands over the inflatable mattress, weighing the pros and cons of sitting down. Her remaining on her feet must be a sign of timidness, just as her silence indicates the same, her pupils carrying the quavering look of someone laboring vigorously to simply keep it together.

"You want some molly?"

She turns around in a flash, demanding it as soon as possible. "Um, yes?"

This wasn't the plan, but when she never sat down, he panicked. His biggest grief and most ludicrous mistake would be to come off as sleazy.

Jameson takes the capsules from a pill bottle in the closet and hands one to Mel. When he does this, he takes his first real look at her. Stupid fucking retard idiot. He hadn't noticed she changed. Earlier she was wearing some funny T-shirt with bicycle shorts, her face scarlet under countless tiny drops of sweat. Now she's in a short lilac dress and black tights, a hole on her knee fixed with clear nail polish, her hair clipped back leaving a trail of Rose perfume. Very pretty. Must mean she cares.

They get glasses of grape juice and swallow the capsules.

"How much is it?" she asks too late.

"I've no idea," he admits. Knowing it comes from Artie, "Probably really strong."

She nods, he blinks. They're both leaning against the counter, watching the microwave clock update itself after a minute.

"That's how I like my drugs."

They smoke a bowl while waiting for it to kick in. The sky reaches its final stage of black as the neighbors settle in for the night. Jameson makes fun of all the pets and their owners.

"Spay, neuter, euthanize," he states. She doesn't necessarily agree, but it's convincing.

Stars move around the dome, the lights of Agoura Hills barely interfering with their sparkle. Coyotes hunt for lost puppies in the wilderness that borders the apartment complex. Cockroaches come out of their hiding spots to surprise you when you get up to use the bathroom. The new friends feel queasy as the first wave distends from their stomachs to their fingers and toes, their tongues unable to express anything remotely as nihilistic as their true selves.

"Fuck!" Mel bellows. "It's cold!" Maybe that's the worst it gets.

Jameson follows her in close behind, halting when she throws herself on the bed and wraps the comforter around herself.

"I wish we could use the TV in the living room, but the HDMI port is broken."

"It only has one?"

"Yeah."

"Is it a smart TV?"

"Yeah."

"Then we could watch Netflix. Or Hulu. I have friends with accounts."

"Accounts," he laughs. "Sure, if you want. I thought maybe we could watch something good. Here." She doesn't respond. "My collection is solid."

She scoots to the edge of the mattress, collecting leftover comforter under her buttocks to provide cushioning. He squats next to her to access his laptop on a bookshelf. In there, Mel notices comic after comic, a Bukowski or two, and a pretzel box containing about fifty 45s.

"Are you feeling a comedy, drama, or horror? Look, here," but she looks away, thinking of something else.

"Does your roommate keep cigarettes in the apartment?"

"What? No, I dunno."

"Sorry. I just really want one."

"There's a gas station up the road."

"I know, but I just want one. I quit smoking some time ago."

"Oh, I see."

"Drugzzz."

"Cray cray."

"Hashtag once in a lifetime."

"Only in Agoura."

"Cali gurlz." He inches his nose without meaning to, his face right by hers, and the impulse occurs to him, but it doesn't overcome him. He gives her time to realize she's uncomfortable and lets her withdraw, pretending to be cracking her neck. Tonight's the night. What does that even mean? "What if we listen to music? Stimulants have a tendency to leave me cross-eyed."

"Sure. Take your pick."

It takes Mel time to find a record. She takes one first, then puts it back when she finds something better. Maybe she's falling in love now, bringing to him the self-titled Velvet Underground. It was all the way at the end. He questions her decision, putting it on nonetheless. They sit in their strange positions until they find themselves cocooned under all the blankets shoulder by shoulder on the floor.

"It's about things that I can't understand yet."

"Yes!" he rumbles. "This might be their best record. I fucking hate Nico."

"For sure. I'm so glad you have this. It's lovely."

"Pale Blue Eyes" takes over and they listen, swaying, their eyes watering. He beams two rows of straight teeth at her through the mirror. She reciprocates.

"Maybe later we could watch something sad."

"Why something sad?"

"To feel better about it. You know? Work on accepting the truth."

"Is that a way of using your time on drugs wisely?"

"I can be detached, get stressed out. But recently I get these surges of—and in a way it should be a sort of happiness—but like, I get reminded several times a day of how evil the world really is. I hadn't ever noticed it before. Most people aren't familiar with anything but their own misery. They only know darkness. I get, um, claustrophobic, I guess. Hunger, sickness, abuse, war, you fucking name it. They're born there in the filth, and they die there in the filth, building crowded little cities of trash. And I'm not talking about having to go so far. It's more common than not." Their eyes meet. "Sorry, I don't mean to...get real."

"No, no, that's...but see, you're never gonna feel better about that. You shouldn't."

"Then I'll never be happy."

"What would you say you want?"

"Less hate...less bigotry?" She frowns. "More. More money. More drugs. More sleep. More, I want more."

"Indulgence."

"You say it like it never brought anyone joy," she grunts.

"Happy overdosing," he says, tipping a make-believe hat.

"I shall."

"I used to indulge, but nah. I'm over it."

"You grew up?"

"You could say I got better. I had to decide to be a good person. One day I started feeling guilt, like, all of a sudden, so everything I did made me feel bad. I had to say fuck it, can't do those things anymore. Gotta be a good person from now on."

"Wow."

"Yeah."

They quit talking for a few seconds, then it extends into some minutes. Mel plays with the soft skin of her elbow. Jameson almost reaches for it to do the same. He touches his and it's not as pleasant as hers looks.

"It really is nice having you around."

"You've mentioned it."

"No, but, like," he traps himself in. He's about to do it and there's no best way to go about it. He might as well be done with it. Just do it. "I like you."

She doesn't play with telling him she likes him too with a hasty, stony smile to state that they are just friends. No. She knows what he means. She shakes her head a little bit, concentrating on her answer. The MDMA sparks out of her hair follicles. The astigmatism settles on her right eye. Her hands itch.

"I'm sorry, I don't—" she drops, unable to finish her convoluted thoughts, causing him to think the worst.

There's no nice way to put the pain that just happened. Vomit goes up his throat. He swallows it.

"I just mean," he says to keep from gagging, "I just wanna keep seeing you...like we have been. But if you don't want to, then we don't have to."

It's simply too soon to put Mel in a tough spot like this one. She thinks of Rodrigo and how she felt that time she slept with him after having slept with someone else—some dude from school who always gave her cigarettes—because Rodrigo didn't want to be her boyfriend. How do you like that? she thought. But she never told him. He did deserve it, but maybe he wouldn't have cared, and instead of feeling foolish at his disinterest unparalleled by her wrath, she figured it would be her secret. It made her feel so nasty she had to cut her hair.

"That's not fair," she squeals. "You're giving me drugs so you can bang me?"

"What? No! No, that's not—"

"So you don't wanna bang me." Shit. That's not fair either.

"Goddammit! You're one of those?"

"One of what?"

"Those guys."

"What guys?"

"Just guys."

"We can be friends," he adds as soon as she looks like she's not gonna speak anymore. "You're just really cool. That's it. We don't have to do anything."

"Everything was great until now. You totally fucking ruined it."

"I ruined it?"

"You ruined it."

"I'm sorry," he says more to himself than to Mel, her face turned in the opposite direction. "I'm rolling so hard right now. I'm sorry."

Mel moves her jaw from side to side so as to not to bite down, grappling the blankets tighter with her hands and feet. Jameson tries to not get emotional, but it wins him over. Tonight's the night. What was he thinking?! The abrupt desperation tumbles his reasoning so cruelly he must run to the bathroom to hide himself, also because he has to go. He tells himself to take it easy, it's got nothing to do with him, but it stings, and he had a large dinner before being struck by the muse of spontaneity, so, you know. He's already told Mel of all his digestive ailments, about his theory that he was born without part of his intestine and everything. She must be understanding.

71

When he comes back, they watch a couple of episodes of *Vice* without saying anything. At the end of "Winners & Losers," she remembers she's got a job interview in the morning, and that seems to be a good reason to leave, saying goodbye from far away, all the way out the door already. Now he begins to get over her.

Mel takes her meds, puts on PJs, and cozies up in her bed. She attempts to use her cell phone as a means of entertainment, but her right eye is completely gone. She's gotta cover it up with one hand and read with the left one, not quite able to use space the same way as before, all blurry and off-center. Eventually she gives up and smokes a bowl. She's coming down now, a bit moody, really tired. Her jaw's gonna hurt like a bitch in the morning.

5

Though the alarm has been expected, it isn't dismissed right away. The unforgiving sun heats up all of Southern California perilously. Not even the dogs wanna go outside to take a dump. Let their masters take care of cute, little mishaps. The postwoman goes up the steep driveway of Kanan Terrace, reminding herself over and over of her children. This is why she does this. People are depending on her. Without any of those responsibilities, Mel dismisses the alarm to get ready for her job interview.

Full of confidence and no practice, she takes her pills and looks up the bus route as she tokes slightly. Rohtos and Especially Escada do the trick of masking her highness. She leaves way too early, and when passing Jameson's apartment, she tries to listen in but nothing's happening.

Had she stayed a second longer, she would have heard the action that was about to start. A loud knock on Jameson's door announces Artie's come home.

"Jameson!" she says, opening it a gap. He grunts. "Jameson, you left your tortillas out."

"What?" he asks, still asleep.

"You left your tortillas out."

"What do you mean I left them out?"

"You left your tortillas out!" she repeats furiously.

"Sorry?"

"It's for your own good I'm telling you. I don't want them to go bad."

He sits up and confronts her, and she thinks this gives her permission to step inside all the way. He shakes his head, rubbing his eyes clean.

"What the fuck are you talking about?"

"You. Left. Your. Tortillas. Out!"

"Yeah, so?"

"So they're gonna go bad. I'm just telling you so—"

"It's shelf food," you fucking tard tart! he bellows inwardly.

"Whatever, dude. Just put them away."

"So what do you want?" he gargles as she's turning away. "Seriously was that—"

"I want you to stop leaving shit out!"

"Is this why you woke me up?"

"It's not my fault you're always sleeping!"

He reaches for his phone and unlocks the screen.

"It's nine forty!"

"Yeah! Exactly!"

"Weren't you in Palm Springs anyway?"

"Life's not a vacation, Jameson!"

How dare she? She shuts Jameson's door with her feeble near to no strength, and though he wants to keep fighting until he's proven right, he's too tired and, most importantly, mature for that shit. Artie's shit. The shit she's always starting due to her habit of being awful. Borderline bitch.

But no, how dare he? She knows what he's thinking. He must be calling her a retard, a bitch, saying she's always starting shit. Fuck him. He's gotten fat, so, you know, karma.

Taking off the sunglasses she left on her head, Artie sets her purse down on the kitchen counter and erases the message she left on the whiteboard on the fridge. The tortillas get her attention once more and she rolls her eyes, dragging her heeled feet to her bedroom where Pollo watches Celeste do her 'mommy's home' dance.

"I thought she was sick yesterday," he says to her.

"Really? Why?" she asks alarmed.

"She looked like she was about to die."

"That's weird."

"Yeah, and now she's all good."

"Thank god."

"Yeah, thank that guy."

Artie's feet give way and she sinks atop dozens of discarded outfits. Pollo pulls her shoes off as a nice gesture, flinging the tan leather Dior pumps in the direction of the closet. Celeste jumps up against the box spring with her paws extended as far as they go. When she's grabbed and deposited on Artie's stomach, she chases her tail before resting where her smell goes right into Artie's nostrils. She's used to it.

With a swift dealer swish, Pollo takes out a Marlboro Red and strikes a match on the bottom of his shoe. The act is rehearsed. One day he got tired of the whole skater boy gets lost in a trailer park thing he was trying to pull off, and he got a new wardrobe, found a hairstylist, and picked up handsome mannerisms. The ladies became more interested in him, but that was only a side effect. Now he just lets people think he's gay. Some in his circle gossip behind his back, but they don't know anything.

Pollo caresses Artie's strawy hair with uttermost sweetness. Nobody knows this side of him. Just her. And as she purrs from her throat in a kind of smile, he thinks he's got her little bit of goodness for himself too.

"I need to move," her voice cracks.

"Don't get upset," he says smoothly with a puff of smoke. "Everything's gonna be okay."

"I don't know." She rubs one of her eyes, smudging eyeliner out of place, until she gets an eyelash out. "I could pay the rent till he gets another roommate if I need to."

"Artie, please. Trust me."

"I keep taking his socks, but it's like he doesn't care someone's after him—"

"I thought it was a prank."

"It was. Until I threw them away. Fucking tired of him. Sleeping all the goddamn time. And now this—"

"I mean it, Artie. Just trust me, you're fine," he spits.

She nods. If anything, she can trust him. And only him.

Quick footsteps outside the door are joined by knocks on Artie's door.

"No smoking inside, dammit!" Jameson cries out with a few more knocks for emphasis.

Dismissing it with a little twirl of the wrist, Artie takes out one of her strawberry Kiss Superslims and lights it in spite.

"Fuck off!" she lets him know through the walls.

Jameson can imagine her in there, smoking more because he told her not to, making herself out to be a victim, stuck with her twin brother and the Chihuahua because no one else likes her.

Unable to get an early start with the medication weighing down on him, Jameson exhales his last breath of enmity and makes his way back to his bed, this time locking the door. Artie's gonna think of whatever she can to call him out on it, but he's got a better method of dealing with her now. At first, when they had just moved in and the 'living together' issues arose, he tried to make note of it all in order to keep Artie pleased—they were great friends, no need to cause problems. Yet as much as she tried to be right, Jameson caught on to her bullshit when she complained about his leaving a dirty pan out on the stove for a week, and it ended up being hers. It was funny because she left him a letter on the white board on the fridge detailing why he was such a good-for-nothing loser, coming back home to a footnote reading: *All this, this is you.* After that, she remembered. She was so enraged that night she cut her wrists, parading the bandages for days in order to blame Jameson. He didn't talk to her until she put on long sleeves.

Before closing his eyes, he texts Mel telling her to break a leg, and just as quickly as he woke up, he falls asleep again, the memory of his confrontation with Artie about to get mixed up with his dreams, so much that he forgets if it really happened.

6

It being his day off, Jameson delays getting up for another hour after officially waking up some time in the afternoon. He switches between the state of being happy warm intertwined up and under his three blankets and the suffocation of eighty-seven-degree weather. He checks his phone and goes through some emails before getting to Mel's text. *killed it, son. i start training friday.* The news please him so well he gets the feeling this might not compare to any previous fancy.

He plays guitar for a few hours, feeling pointless, his talent wasted. He smokes half a bowl, then another half, wishing he had that Xanax. In the kitchen, he checks the fridge to see what he can eat. If only he had someone to cook for. Instead, he lackadaisically unwraps a Trader Joe's TV dinner and sticks it in the microwave. When it's no longer scalding, he works his way through most of it while the Booker T. and the M.G.'s record he got for eight bucks at Record Outlet spins with a few pops here and there.

"Mel! Dinner!"

The steak stink lingers in the whole apartment, but Mel isn't high enough to want it yet. Not feeling it, she sits across from Herman and watches him dig the knife eagerly, biting it off the fork with his teeth on the metal. The sound nearly pierces Mel's ears.

"I had a nightmare this morning," she starts in order to avoid the food for now, "about this huge, rabbit-like, kangaroo-ish animal thing that gets trapped in the basement of my house during a storm. The whole place floods and this creature is in the dark startled out of its mind. I can barely see it, but I'm trying to save it. And everyone else who's there, like friends and family, none of them help out even though the whole place is falling apart. So I get horribly angry at them, trying really hard to get the animal outta there, and eventually I do, so I ride it out of the house, and I watch everything get crumpled and washed away, and I'm grieving because I loved them all, but I feel like I got something better out of it. And then I just keep riding the animal through an apocalyptic world where everyone's out to get you. I don't remember the rest so well 'cause then I woke up and stuff, but that first part, it was...intense. Especially since I don't normally dream anymore."

"You don't?" Mel shakes her head. "You used to dream so much when you were little. You could lucid dream in kindergarten."

"Yeah, I could fly out of any situation."

"And sometimes you had repetitive dreams, too."

"Losing my shoes."

"Losing your shoes, yeah," he repeats, cutting another piece of steak. "Showing up to the movies naked. Not finding the right outfit."

"That one was the worst one."

"They could get scary. I would hear you whimper or scream in the middle of the night."

"You used to give me cough syrup to make me go to sleep," she says sourly.

"You were fine. And it was only once. When you were seven or eight and your cousin showed you *The Texas Chain Saw Massacre*."

"Wes?"

"Yeah."

"He showed me that when I was little? He was so odd..."

"You couldn't sleep and you didn't let anyone else sleep either. Also you had gotten hurt that day. You fell or something. It was so stressful. You even called your mom and she was being a..."

Mel plays with a piece of steak on her fork before eating it.

"You know what?" she says with the food in her mouth. "I'm not really that hungry." She gets up with the plate and leaves it on the counter. "I'll have it later."

Herman's cell phone starts to ring as Mel pours herself a glass of water. Then a knock on the door.

"It's Laura," he says excitedly, bringing himself to his feet.

Seeing this as the perfect opportunity to ditch out, Mel waits the thirty seconds it takes Herman to welcome his guest in, sending a little wave in Laura's direction and a, "How are ya?" before disappearing into her room with a mild headache.

She pops six Buspars and half an Ativan, then wastes time on Instagram as they begin to take effect, one stalking leading to another, ending up on Artie's private account. All she has to do is click the follow button, wait for her decision, and if all goes well, take a peek into her life. But Mel could never.

The knuckles on her left hand itch a little, then more. It must be dusty in here, the skin quickly becoming hard and pink. Trying to ignore the nuisance, Mel smokes a bowl, thinking she wants to go to bed early. Yet another bowl doesn't do the trick either. She's hoping she'll get used to the medication, because while being pumped-up all day should help her get shit done, it's only making her uncomfortable. The anorexia, the anxiety, the insomnia, all heightened.

Her mother calls to check up on everything Mel was supposed to do, make sure she's all right. The day they said goodbye, it wasn't on great terms, so much they've only been texting about crucial things like *at dad's* and *okay*.

"Yo, is it true Dad gave me cough syrup to go to sleep after my cousin showed me *The Texas Chain Saw Massacre*?"

"Yeah," says Mom through a yawn. "You were still in shock and you were all hurt and your dad wouldn't even tell me why. It was Carine who called me."

"Yeah, he said you were a bitch about it."

"Probably," Mom admits. "It was a tough summer, that one. It was...it was hard to let you go back to those people. But listen, I really gotta go. I'm super hungry, and I just got home from work, and I'm super tired, and I—"

"Okay, okay."

"And Melaina," she pauses for dramatic effect, "go to the gym."

"'Kay, bye."

"Bye."

Mel hangs up relieved and puts away the cell phone in an attempt to stop dealing with people today. She takes off her jeans, used tissues falling out of the pockets, and puts *Pendulum* on. It appears she's staying in.

In the living room, Herman hands Laura a beer and they sit to watch something together. He notices she seems distracted, and he's wondering whether she showed up like this for a specific reason. He would ask what happened, but Laura doesn't like being questioned. She has a lot of these quirks like no peeing in front of each other and leaving her relationship status on Facebook blank. Whatever it all means, he's willing to overlook it as long as it doesn't get personal. For example, Laura doesn't brush her teeth every night. She doesn't floss or use mouthwash either. Now this could lead Herman, the son of a dentist, into intolerableness. But so far it just irritates him somewhat.

Tonight keeps progressing as an ordinary one—Herman brushes his teeth, Laura looks at herself in the mirror as she takes off her clothes. They get in bed and say nothing. He gives her some time before closing his eyes. She's never just come over like this before.

"I've reconsidered," she blurts out.

"What?" he asks, pleased with himself.

"Herman," she says, pausing as if it's a glaring, silly thing, "I've reconsidered what you asked me."

"You mean—"

"Yeah."

"You wanna..."

"Move, yeah! And let's not wait. I'll start moving my things as soon as possible."

"Laura," he whispers.

"I know."

His breathing is interrupted when the tear ducts begin to flow. She scratches the back of his neck with her long, slightly dirty nails. Though she tries to not find it annoying, she really can't stand it when he cries, putting her in a role she's never been asked to play before, being of the fairer sex and all. Nonetheless, let that remain her insecure little secret. The woman isn't as heartless as to tell him this is why she took so long to change her mind, why, even now after just having agreed, she doesn't truly want to live with him. It would mean giving up the few things she has like her independence and, well, yes, her independence. Forty-years-old, it will be the first time Laura moves in with a boyfriend. Herman found it concerning at first, but all he could do was roll with it. He can't expect the same from every one of his middle-aged peers: the scorn compiling atop last year's through a veil of unfaithfulness, greed, and routine, not knowing who you— you!—are anymore, twice married, twice divorced.

"I'm so happy," he tells her without thinking whether it's real or if it's just one of those moments.

Their intimate embrace gets soaked in Herman's tears. The ickiness keeps bothering Laura, so she proceeds to kiss him where he's dry, shutting him up with some of them seductive moves. She takes over and screws him more avidly than they're used to, determined to keep whatever she thinks she's gonna lose.

When she gets off him, Laura falls asleep quicker than he's supposed to. She snores a little bit, something they're definitely gonna have to talk about. And maybe it's time to tell her about the pills, too, then he can take them in front of her since skipping a dose means he won't get any sleep. But it's too soon for that now. Too late. He'd rather just close his eyes and wait.

One of his legs goes stiff, so he turns on his side, putting a pillow between his thighs like the doctor said. But then that doesn't work out so he turns on his other side, repeating the cycle for as long as he can.

Four in the morning. It must be ticking close to four in the morning.

Herman turns his head and reads his clock: three fifteen. Yup. Nearing four in the morning.

He stretches his legs, scratches his arm under all that hair, and, making sure to be as silent as possible, he gets up from the bed. His knees crack. Laura exhales heavily at these sounds. He envies her ability to not wake up with all this going on.

As soon as he's out of the room, he lets his socks make that rasping sound all the way to the bathroom where he relieves himself of four hours worth of piss. His eyes are their normal size once he looks in the mirror. It shows how little he's slept. It'd be ridiculous to take a Valium now, so instead he pops two Benadryls.

"Holy shit!" he shrieks under his breath upon opening the door. Mel is standing there in front of her room, half her face in the dark. "What are you doing?"

"Going to the bathroom," she answers, pointing out to him the obviousness of his own reasons.

"Go to sleep," he tells her when he reaches his room.

She waits for him to be gone before entering the bathroom. It's the third time she's gotten up to pee. It's clear each time, too, like she's producing more urine than usual.

"Polyuria," she utters, looking at her cell phone screen. She must have polyuria.

Her hand itches and she scratches it in deep, long strokes like she's been doing all night, trying to get distracted, trying to forget the unholy sounds coming from the other side of the apartment. She dithers.

At this time, the building complex is quiet. There might not be one person still up. Those that lie awake in bed don't count for sometimes that's all of us. And we remain muted, foreseeing that eternal rest, working without sleep, walking around undead. Some even get restless leg syndrome.

Hypochondria overcomes Mel, and the indecent incident of having heard Laura having sex with her father gets buried in the back of her mind where she can forget about it. The marijuana she so obediently smokes helps with these things. Some people drink, others binge, sometimes purge, smoke, toke, poke, poker, crush, rush, blow it up on plush, help the needy, needy addicts, whatever you can think of.

She works her way out of WebMd and onto Instagram where she posts a video she took earlier of a dying moth, then moves on to look at her friends' uploads. Almost instantly, she sees the orange notification: a like from Jameson.

you up? she texts.

yeah.

There's not a good way to go about seeing him. The night's past ripe. What would they even do? Yeah, I know, smoke weed and watch TV. Is that worth her effort? She would have to make it sound all like nothing bad ever happened between them, and they're great friends, and only friends, and they should keep being friends till the end of time.

The problem with having these ideas is that Mel does actually like Jameson. He's pretty cool. He doesn't seem like a dickhead trying to get with her just because that's his only use for girls. Yet there's evidence that supports the opposite. She used to have an easy time telling men apart, but once she was played, there existed no more means to go by. Were she to point out what she's iffy about, first of all, they just met. Second, he's already coming on strong. And third, even if his intentions are pure, she's so mixed up about all this stuff, she'd end up mercilessly breaking his heart.

Although—she thinks analytically—if she could just get over herself once and for all, Jameson does have a lot going for him. He's friendly, easy to talk to, deep, handsome, and he smells like an empty room with white curtains being blown by the breeze of an open window.

can i apologize in person? she sends after thinking about it, still feeling guilty about ending the previous night so suddenly when she could have communicated a bit better. Waste of molly.

i don't know what you'd be apologizing for, but you can come over if you want.

Excitement pulls Mel out of bed. She takes off her dirty T-shirt and puts on a clean one, looks for her shorts until she realizes she hasn't shaved, and then has trouble finding her jeans under the bed. Before putting them on, she changes her underwear—no VPL, thank you very much—and puts on socks, the knee ones with little gnomes on them. It takes her another minute to rustle the tips of her fingers against her scalp and sneak an Altoid in her mouth, then charges towards Jameson's on a mission.

"I kind of have a thing that's not resolved yet," she bursts in as soon as she's able to, her hands itchier by the second.

"Oh."

"Yeah, it's, uh, just something that's not officially over. For now."

Jameson turns on the light and yawns. This is not the face of someone who's manic and wired, more like depressed and tired. She wants to apologize for bothering him, but she already has to explain herself for something else, which is like being sorry except not exactly so.

"Good luck with that," he says, earnestly forlorn.

His talking lagging, mouth open, white T-shirt stained, the young man blinks about ten times before processing what's going on. He'd just gone to the bathroom for a while, and we all know what to do then: Instagram. He regretted telling her he was up forthwith, but then he heard the knocks on his window and there was no going back.

"I didn't mean to be mean," Mel says when it appears she's got his attention.

"It's really not a big deal."

"Cool. Cool. 'Cause...you know how it is."

"Sure, yeah."

"It's just not the right time right now."

"Don't worry about it."

"I feel really bad."

"There's nothing to feel bad about."

"But I do."

"It's seriously okay."

She nods, crossing her arms, scratching. "Sorry I'm acting weird."

"You're not acting...in any way."

"Well, you don't really know me. And plus: 'you met me at a very strange time in my life.'"

"I understand," he presses on, shifting from one foot to the other in the middle of the living room. "It's all new."

"It is! And—and now I'm also on this medication—"

"Medication?" he asks without thinking, now fearing she's gonna take it the wrong way.

"Yeah, I'm, uh," she shrugs and inhales, looking at the floor, "I'm bipolar."

Randy crickets chirp so loud that Jameson takes a moment to appreciate their calls. Something so vulgar, something so refined. The girl he likes is telling him his own secrets, and he'd rather not pay attention. But the fucks of nature remind him even more of what's going on. Mel scratches her elbow. She must be soft. He's got a lot to say now that he thinks about it. Where to begin is the question.

"Same." Somewhere in there, he thinks he sees her expression change for the better, but her hair is all in her face. "I knew there was something off about you as soon as we met."

"Fuck you," she titters, trying to hide her mouth.

"I'm not saying it's a bad thing. I mean, it is. But I like you, don't I?"

"I'm not offended. I'm just surprised."

"Don't be. It's the bipolar magnet. Part of the package."

"Ha."

"Think about it. Think about how many bipolar people you have in your life."

"Whoa."

"And it stretches to other shit too. We get all the weirdos. Sociopaths, narcissists, borderlines."

"Junkies."

"The eating disordered."

"Cutters, thieves, promiscuou...tors?"

"That's my friends."

"And family."

"Everyone's got something."

"We got the same thing. That's hilarious."

"It's not a great thing to be proud of," he reminds her.

"Oh, I wouldn't have it any other way. Sometimes I forget who I am because I forget that I'm not my disease. It's a mood disorder. It's not even a personality disorder. And it's not what powers me. I am just as—if not more—creative when I'm not freaking the fuck out puking all my emotions through an endless roller coaster ride. But even then, I wouldn't have it any other way."

"That's because you're bipolar."

"I know," she sighs, pulling her bangs aside, revealing her countenance, coming to a realization. "This is why you were on your balcony smoking weed."

"Wouldn't have it any other way."

Since she doesn't say anything, he leads her to his room. He opens up his laptop and finds the *Vice* folder, putting an episode on when she looks at what he's doing and doesn't protest. He sits under the covers and offers her the other half of the bed. She sits and pulls the covers over her legs in order to remove her jeans, which she does against her better judgment, glad she's opting for comfort.

Artie's gone for the night so they smoke inside. He'll have enough time when he wakes up to air out the room. Besides, it's not that she'd mind, it's that he does. So who cares? This show is more bearable this way.

Jameson knows he's about to pass out about five minutes into the second half. To his relief, Mel's eyelids flutter. By the time the episode ends, they're both practically completely gone. No one turns off the TV or closes the laptop. The two fall asleep just as the other two do.

7

"You're the first girl I sleep with that I don't have sex with," he says, shifting positions to not get his morning breath in the way.

"You're terrible." Jameson and Mel look into each other's dark brown eyes, leaning on their sides on the inflatable mattress. She rubs the dried rheum off her eyes while he restrains himself from kissing her. It's kinda nice, what he just said. "You say those things and then expect me to not think you're one of those guys."

"I'm not."

"Whatever."

"And why would I have any reason to sleep with girls, anyway? You go around sleeping with guys?"

"I dunno, I'm sure it's happened before."

Neither of them knows what time it is. Mel turned out to be very tossy-turny, but they still spooned a few times in both directions. And even with the anxiety they were both harvesting in their stomachs, they managed to sleep pretty well.

"I'm the least douchy guy you'll ever meet. You just don't see it yet."

"It takes time to earn someone's trust. Even if you happen to be the most perfect man ever, I'm gonna be watching you very closely for years," she lets him know sternly. "Also because: men."

"I feel you. If I were a woman, I would never leave my apartment. I'd be a virgin with some cats."

"That's actually a lot of girls I know."

"Is there a group of scientists somewhere in the world working on how to not need men anymore? Every bad thing that happens, oh yeah, men."

"That's how you know god created man first. Oh, never mind, I get it now. And then there were women."

"I wish we could just fall out of evolution. Become pointless. Then there'd be a progressive, compassionate world," he says, starting to yawn.

"That's why I believe in dualism. Half men, half women."

"Good and evil balancing themselves out."

"Yeah, but I wonder...'cause psychos are born. They are one percent of the population no matter what. But are there people born inherently good? Like, is there a percentage for that? Or are we born evil? Original sin. You gotta work towards being good. You face decisions that question your morality and then you act."

"Around sixth or seventh grade, kids were horrible. These two boys from my class set a goddamn cat on fire. What were they thinking? What's gonna happen? You can sort of figure that out before trying it. I mean, the cat just burned to death. So why?"

"To test themselves."

"But, see, I knew that was wrong, and I would have never thought of doing something like that. Maybe not so much morally but because I thought it was stupid, but either way, I was better than them."

"Yeah, I mean, the other thing going on is that maybe kids are born innocent," she starts.

"And they're corrupted," he finishes for her.

"Exactly. That's why when I think about it, there are two opposing forces working together. Yeah, every day there's a new school shooting and someone gets raped on their way home from work, but there's flowers and music, I guess."

"It's hard to remember that."

"Yeah, when I think about it, I wonder: am I good, or am I just not being evil?"

"Only you know. Everyone has their own code, but good and evil can't really be argued. Our mental disorder still gives us choice. It's not like the insane. Or, think about it, pedophiles are in nature attracted to children, dude, and that's one issue no one addresses. What do you do with those people? Even those who don't wanna hurt kids, even they admit sometimes it's just a matter of time. Or they watch child pornography. That's not a victimless crime. But we're not even close to understanding them and helping them out."

"No one's gonna wanna help a child molester. People are still weird about anyone who is willing to admit they have a mental illness. But there's still a sliver of choice. You should be able to control yourself no matter how dreary it gets. It's when you give in and say fuck it that you have a problem."

"Well, also 'cause good isn't all that contagious. I don't know anyone that donates significant amounts of money. But indulging, that's, I mean, that's what a regular human being does. I used to indulge a lot. You know, drugs. And I don't think there's anything wrong in doing drugs, I love drugs, but it doesn't necessarily do good to lead a lifestyle that's just that, every one of your actions directed towards getting loaded. You can't choose to not be part of society anymore. You can't be half-awake. That's dehumanizing," he lets out fast, cracking his knuckles.

"And when you think about all that went down in order for you to get those drugs, too, that hurts, man. But it's still not enough to keep me from doing them. Humans have been getting high since they figured out how. That's not gonna change. And I don't want it to," she says, giving him her hand to crack her fingers for her. "If it weren't for drugs, I wouldn't be so understanding. Doing acid is what brought me to these conclusions. Forces of good and evil working together. And time! I feel time differently. Like I'm in the fourth dimension or something. It's all happening at the same time, my birth, my death, everything, and then I'm not afraid anymore, and that feeling stays with me for a while, a few months, until I get all depressed again."

"Just do more acid," he suggests, cracking the last finger.

"But then I'd lose my mind and all that work would be useless once I'm setting cats on fire. I gotta pee."

She finds her jeans by her feet and pulls on them, causing the green sticky note that was in her back pocket from days ago to fall out. Because she doesn't remember what it is, she opens it up: *Dear Jameson, nice meeting you. Sorry I was weird. I wasn't feeling too hot. I'm new and I don't know anyone, so let's be friends. Sincerely, Mel.*

"Aww."

Jumpy, she turns to see Jameson sitting up reading over her shoulder.

"Give a girl some privacy," she mumbles, flushing.

"You shoulda given it to me. Means a lot."

Causing her to smile, he takes the note and rereads it while she puts her pants on, her ass briefly hanging out, and steps out. She gets to the bathroom, but it's occupied. A minute later,

Artie comes out with neatly applied makeup and straightened hair. She's taken aback by Mel's tall frame standing there right in her face and walks past her without saying anything.

"Hi," Mel says, waving a bit.

"Hi." Artie lifts her head and they stare at each other for a while. Mel gets that feeling again, like she's seen her before. What movie was it?! Meanwhile, Artie keeps her eyes on her, her thumb moving the pendant hanging from her neck up and down the chain, the Chihuahua trembling in fear behind her. Did she just pee with the dog in the bathroom? "You need anything?" she asks confused.

"No, sorry. I like your shirt."

Artie looks down at her chest. It's her *Evil Dead II* cut-up crop top. "Thanks," she says, waiting for Mel to move first.

"I'm Mel, by the way."

"Yeah, I know."

"You know?" Mel steps forward, her eyes wide.

"Jameson told me," Artie explains. "I'm sure he told you who I am."

"Artie."

"That's right."

"I really like you guys' band. Jameson showed me a few tracks," although, honestly, she found Artie's singing too perfect. Colon, dash, slash.

"Nice. Come here, Celeste," she says, grabbing her dog.

"I love the band name. Night Mara. Has a certain je ne sais quoi, non? You came up with it?" Artie nods. "How did you come up with that?" She shrugs, her lips parting. "Can't wait to be you guys' number one fan."

Without another word, Artie escapes to her room. That's when Mel remembers she needs to pee pretty bad. She remains seated on the toilet when she's done, thoughts connecting in her mind, becoming ideas.

Waking up Jameson, who had no trouble drifting back to sleep, Mel grabs her giant purse and goes through it madly.

"What is it?" he asks. She nods, her arm lost out of sight, as if it were an answer. "Well, what?"

"There's something I want you to take a look at because it's driving me crazy." At last, after all that rummaging, she retrieves a hard piece of paper that she keeps in her hands, staring at it for a long while. She scratches in between her fingers, then makes intense eye contact with Jameson. "Please help my head stop hurting," and she hands him the Polaroid.

"That's you," he says in a cute manner, pointing at her child face. "Cool shirt."

"Yeah, but...just look at it and tell me if you see anything that...bothers you."

"Bothers me?"

"Well, no, it bothers me, I guess."

He brings it up close as if trying to find the differences between this and another imaginary copy.

"I'm not sure," he says. "Looks like you're not having a lot of fun."

"But what about her jewelry?"

"What do you mean?"

She points at the other girl's neck, the small detail he hadn't noticed.

"That."

"Is it..." His eyes go from side to side. "That's like Artie's. But that's not..." And then he sees it. "Is that Pollo?"

"Who—who's Pollo?"

"But that can't—that's not Artie."

"Who's Pollo?" she asks him exasperated.

"Artie's twin brother."

"What does he look like?"

Jameson takes out his cell phone faster than he can process the information and pulls up Artie's Instagram—mostly consisting of restaurant food and duck-faced selfies—scrolling until he finds a picture of Pollo chilling by the pool wearing a fishing hat and wayfarers, a deer tattoo showing on his left deltoid.

"Mh," she studies it. "Pollo, you said? Like Apollo? Artemis and Apollo?"

"Yeah, but...damn...how did you even see that?"

"I—"

"How do you even know them?"

"That's the thing—"

"Samuel B.? What the fuck?"

"Yeah, 'cause that's the thing," she says on top of him to slow him down. "It's not Artie and...Pollo...it's Tilly and Sam."

"Tilly?" He straightens up as she scoots closer to him. "What?"

"Tilly and Sam," she repeats, poking their noses.

"Artie and Pollo though."

"Artie and Pollo though indeed."

She kicks the covers off, the room getting hotter with the topic of conversation. They look at the photo intrigued out of their human ability to reason, starting sentences that get stuck in the dryness of their mouths.

"When I was little, I made everyone call me Bruno 'cause I didn't like Jameson. It lasted about a year," he lets out after waiting for a significant amount of time in which no more information was presented.

"Bruno...that's a good one." Her eyes go somewhere else, leaving a blank look on her face, while he does his best to meet them. "The weird part is, shit, I dunno, it's that I—I don't remember. Any of it. I...none," she goes, blinking spastically, running out of things to say, waving as if to make her problems go away.

"Hey, are you all right?" he asks loudly, giving Mel a fright. She thinks he's asking about her mental state, to which she replies with a so-so movement of the head, until he points at the raw, bumpy rash spreading from her knuckles to the palms of her hands. "That wasn't there before."

Mel inspects them closely. Upon staring at them, they begin to itch again just like they've been doing. She scratches with a nail down the side of her thumb to her wrist, leaving a trail of inflamed skin behind, blood dots poking out.

Without further ado, Jameson hurries Mel into the Cavalier and drives her to Dr. Geyser's office. After a wait of sixteen minutes, which he spends listening to the BBC radio, Mel comes out with a calmer look on her face.

"It's rare, but a small percentage of people who take it get a life-threatening rash from Lamictal," Mel repeats for Jameson just as the psychiatrist said. "Always the one percent. Can't believe I'm not rich."

Starting today, she must go off the mood stabilizer cold turkey. She wonders if it'll help ease her libido, the one side effect she can't counterattack with weed unlike the lack of hunger and tiredness, leaving her in a more dangerous state: high and horny.

And that's exactly what they do when they get back, smoke a bowl and throw quick glances in each other's direction, a mix of 'hard to get' and 'take me' going back and forth. He's not gonna do anything, having learned his lesson. She's aware of that. But there's no rush, especially when there's other stuff to take care of.

Mel goggles the pendant from the kitchen, Artie sprawled on the couch watching *Pretty Wild* with a vodka tonic. She laughs her ass off, the Chihuahua jumping on her torso. "Stop," she tells it. "Celeste, come on," but the dog doesn't get it. "Fucking Jesus!" and she spills. Jameson stops midway from flipping a burger to give her a deadly stare. "Fuck you." Counting in his head, Jameson turns back around and keeps cooking. "Who's the apple of my eye? Who's the best listener? You, Celeste! You! The only one I can trust. The only one."

Upon hearing that, Jameson rolls his eyes, grinding his teeth. Mel tells him to relax and he nods excessively, having trouble doing so. He takes two hamburger buns and spreads them on paper plates. She pours some ketchup and mustard, and he gets the turkey patties from the pan. He adds cheese, grilled onions, and closes them up, handing one to Mel. They consider eating at the dinner table just to change their mind when Artie's cell phone rings, and she answers with the meanest hello.

"It's her mom," Jameson says after closing his bedroom door. "When she answers like that, you know it's her mom."

"I miss my mom. But I think she's still mad at me. She got jealous that I wanted to come live with my dad. It's immature, but I get it. I mean, honestly, if it weren't for you, I would have probably already gone back."

"Thanks for making the sacrifice."

"You don't know how long it's been since I can talk to someone. You know, I...I really appreciate honesty. That's probably what I care about the most. I'm a truthful person. The whole bipolar thing doesn't go too well with it 'cause it makes me look indecisive. What? Can't I change my mind? I'm not gonna always be right the first time. Some things take some thought."

He agrees. They work on their burgers for a while before putting on a record. Mel chooses *I Never Loved a Man the Way I Love You* and doesn't hide her intentions. They cuddle with only the Christmas lights on, holding on tighter and inching in closer, her lips on his neck, a wet peck, their souls light ablaze, devouring each other's faces, all night long, hands strong, moving up the bases. For the first time in years, they fall asleep without extra help.

8

Waking up now with a headache, it's officially been a week of
an all-consuming cleansing to get the poison out of Mel's

system. Even though it was a very small dose, she withdrew crazily, going off on Jameson over the stupidest things. She even said she would never see him again, the selfish bastard. All he had done was forgotten to tell her he was going out with his brother later one day when they were hanging out. Apparently she had gotten the impression that they were gonna spend the night together, and it had been inconsiderate of him to lead her on like that if he was just gonna leave. I dunno, something like that. She landed her foot inside his television, and somehow he forgave her, making her question if she would ever do the same for him. Although before the incident she wouldn't have, she had to change her mind about that and a lot of other things when he accepted her apology and couldn't wait to get along with her again. Because being on good terms simply wasn't enough for her, she bought him an HD projector with money she didn't have, her credit card coming in handy.

But even after that, Mel's just not the same. Jameson does his best to tolerate her mood swings, yet when she sits quietly staring at nothing for long periods of time, he gets concerned. She says she's been thinking too much, and it shows. No attention, all anticipation, and she paces, paces, paces.

"No, I've never met their mom," Jameson answers about the Waltz twins for the tenth time. "But for what Artie says about her, she's a bitch."

Meanwhile in Artie's room, something smells like dog shit. Jameson doesn't know where it's coming from. Mel would rather not find out. The dog has been gone as long as its owner, so at least it must be getting fed. Artie probably isn't. When she's gone this long, it's no good news. If it weren't for the note she left on the whiteboard on the fridge saying she was going on retreat, Jameson would have guessed she was murdered. She didn't answer her phone, showed no activity on any social medium, and even her brother didn't know where she was. Mel had seen the grown up version of the boy in the Polaroid hanging around the building complex looking rather unkempt. She almost waved at him before remembering that she didn't actually know him.

This yes-but-no nonsense keeps giving Mel migraines. A flash of light distracts her vision to the left, but that's just Jameson lifting a dirty towel with his shoe.

"Here it is," he says, and the stench wafts through the room.

Mel turns around perplexed. "What?"

"The shit," he answers, pointing at it.

"Oh. Ew," Mel's voice shakes. "Just leave it."

"I'm not gonna leave it, Jesus! Week-old feces! I live here, goddammit!"

Not wanting to take it out on Mel, Jameson goes to the kitchen to get the necessary cleaning products. She keeps searching in every drawer from back to front, top to bottom, for anything incriminating that would explain who Artie really is. So far a double-ended dildo and a pill bottle full of Adderall prescribed to an Erica Lowry are self-explanatory, just like the handful of addies Mel shoves in her pocket, one of them already going down her esophagus.

"Do you know an Erica Lowry?"

"No," Jameson answers as he kneels down, his gloved hands about to handle the poop situation. "But I know a Danielle Lowry."

"Does she have a sister or something?"

"I dunno. Maybe. I wasn't friends with Danielle, but she was in my P.E. class, I think. What does it matter?"

"Gotta find out who this Erica is."

"Look, Mel, like Artie says herself," he starts, gearing up to imitate the girl in question, "Artie parties."

Mel grimaces without looking away from her investigation. The bedside table, the vanity table, the dresser, the bookcase, under the bed, all clear. There's only one more place to check: the closet. If this is the room, she doesn't wanna know what state the closet is in. With trembling hands, Mel opens it, a black see-through blouse and its hanger falling from the top shelf and onto her face.

"Why doesn't Artie just live in Hollywood?" Mel asks, watching him put the turd in a bag.

"She doesn't actually go to trendy clubs or wherever she acts like she goes. All these nice clothes and shit...the only place she goes is Palm Springs. And even there, when she took me once, I was surprised at how lonely they are. It's just sad. They're not hanging out with Clay fucking Easton or whatever. They just live from restaurant to restaurant. That's all they do. Drugs and food," and he gets up to throw the crap away.

"Sounds like they got it all figured out."

"Gluttony is what it is."

A single row of dresses takes up half of the closet, these ranging from the trashiest, fitted, glittery kind to the classiest of little black dresses arranged in no particular order, some hanging from one side only and plenty forgotten atop the shoes underneath. Mel pushes the dresses aside looking behind them where Artie's left some boxes and bags. She pulls out a plastic bag with magazine cut-outs in it, sets it aside, takes out a shoe box with, who would have guessed, shoes inside, puts it down. The other half of the closet is mostly dedicated to coats and blouses. Here she finds an unopened two-for-one box of enemas, a half-burnt cinnamon candle the size of her foot, and a Louis Vuitton cosmetic carrier. Upon opening this last item, Mel finds what she's been looking for.

"Here it is!" she says enthusiastically as he gets down to spray the carpet, flipping through all sorts of legal documents, photocopies, bills, setting one of them aside between her pinky and ring finger.

"Let me see."

She holds it out to him, giving him time to read. "Artemis and Apollo. Didn't you ever think that was odd?" she mumbles while he reads the birth certificate.

"I figured they had the worst parents, yeah. But I never thought they changed their names."

The cleaning product fizzes as it attaches itself to the beige hairs of the carpet, Jameson giving the matter more thought.

"They gotta be hiding something. I got a strange vibe from her, like, the second I met her."

"Yeah, you've told me—"

"I seriously felt physically ill, like someone shook my brain inside my head, Magic 8 Ball style. Almost threw up on your doorstep—"

"I get it, jeez," he says, disliking the way she talks about his friend. "This makes no sense—"

"I know it doesn't make sense. Why would she act like she doesn't know me if she does? She asked you who I was and you told her—"

"I said you were Melanie."

"Same thing."

"But you asked me about Artie and you don't know where you know her from either."

"Yeah, but it's, uh…" Mel trails off, another flash from the corner of her eye frightening her. "I gotta go to the eye doctor. Or maybe it's a tumor…"

"Mel," Jameson says, putting his hand on her shoulder. She shakes it off as she tends to. Besides the fact that they've had sex thrice—something they're both pretending isn't a big deal, still a debatable reoccurrence given his habit of leaving on his socks—she doesn't let him touch her the rest of the time, saying she doesn't like much physical contact. "We're gonna figure this out." She nods and withdraws, standing up. Defeated, he remains so.

With nowhere else to look, Mel goes to the door ready to leave when Jameson makes a sound. "What?" she asks. He points. "What?"

She follows his finger, but he gets to the vanity table faster. "This," he mutters, sticking his hand underneath the right drawer where the corner of a sheet of paper is showing, a piece of tape hanging uselessly from it. "Maybe it came off when you opened the drawer." He gently removes the other edges and brings it forth. Mel gets on his level as he opens it, revealing a list of about ten names, all of them written using a different pen or pencil, a few of them crossed out.

"Or maybe it was placed—or replaced—recently," she says, pausing at the last one: *Neighbor.*

Jameson gets up and washes his hands, leaving Mel there for a while before she notices that with this, she's done here.

Artie's bedroom door is closed for good. Mel sits on the couch and studies the hit list. Jameson takes out the box of mini pancakes from the freezer and places twenty on a paper plate.

"At least you're not on here," she says, tapping on the penultimate, crossed out Sara Johnston.

"Maybe she changed her name for artistic reasons."

"Matilda Bonham isn't too bad. Tilly and Sam," she exhales, twisting her fingers in off-putting positions by her ears. "Tilly and Sam."

"She probably got busted for something that ruined her reputation."

"Clearly." Mel massages her temples, feeling a brutal headache coming on. "And she's hiding out here."

"This is starting to scare the shit out of me," he laughs.

"Dude! Imagine how I feel!" He places the plate in the microwave and sets the timer, stepping away from the radiation and into Mel's personal space. She takes a step backward. "I had that nightmare again. The one about the mara."

"Would you say you had a night mara?"

"Yes, Jameson, it's funny every time," she half chortles, half fed up. "Ah! There it goes again!" A flash in the corner of her eye interrupts her train of thought. "This is seriously starting to get freaky."

The microwave beeps, and Jameson retrieves the paper plate, setting it on the table so he can shove half of them onto another plate. Mel takes a banana from the fruit bowl and cuts some onto Jameson's plate, the rest onto hers.

"Don't we have some chicken salad left over from yesterday?" he asks, causing them both to raise their eyebrows.

He checks the fridge and brings the container over. Mel pours honey over her pancakes. When she's done, Jameson does the same. They've been having breakfast together every day for the past week. They go to the grocery store and fake fight over who's paying. As much as he would like to afford it, Jameson sometimes has to let her get it. His job waiting tables at a fine dining restaurant isn't enough to feed two mouths.

"I work at three thirty today," he says, gulping down a large bite.

"What?! That's in half an hour."

"Yeah, that's why we gotta hurry."

Mel shoves food in her mouth as she goes to Jameson's room to find her black pants and black shirt on her shelf in his closet. He follows a few seconds after, also looking for his black pants and black shirt. They stand by each other in the bathroom doing their hair, Jameson gelling it, Mel collecting it into a taut ponytail. Because she doesn't have a car and since the movie theater is four blocks from the restaurant, Jameson drives both of them to work. On days like today when he goes in two hours before Mel's shift, she waits at the Barnes and Noble next door.

After being there for a while, Mel checks her watch, cringing each time the hour approaches. Curved on the floor of the bookstore, using her purse for back support, she opens Artie's list. *Neighbor,* yeah, yeah, it could be anyone, but especially her, the new neighbor. Melanie, neighbor, she answers to a lot of things. Her chest pounds with anxiety. Not another panic attack, please.   .

But what about Sara Johnston? Second to last and taken care of. She searches for her on Facebook, Instagram, Twitter, all of them, but it just so happens that there's too many Sara Johnstons in the world, none of them in the area.

A few of the other names seem to have been written in a frenzy, making the scribbles hard to decipher, the rest too vague unaccompanied by surnames. Those she understands, she searches for, coming up with three sure finds: Renata Klein gets plenty of likes on symmetrical, washed up 16:9 shots of rooms; Kay Ursula has to abbreviate her political wrath by using *ur* and *ppl;* and Vinnie Beck has a whole In Memoriam page to his name with over 1,500 members.

That's it. She killed him. 1991-2009. The deleted profile of a Til Nil having posted at the very bottom, short and sweet: *I'll miss you forever. See you in heaven.*

It's not that she runs out of ideas, mostly Mel simply runs out of the ability to interpret her thoughts logically, and thus she gets distracted today by starting the *Girls* graphic novel series. She goes through the first few pages without a problem, but then a shadow blinds her right eye completely for a moment, and not a quick one either. It's like the flashes, only instead of thinking oh my god, paparazzi, it's more like oh my god, the grim reaper. She takes note of which page she's on and closes the book, burying her face in between her knees. A non-binary teenager browsing the manga section feels better about themselves upon finding the ailing girl on the ground.

When it's time to go to work, Mel gets up from her almost-nap and has trouble maintaining her balance on her way to the escalator. The ride down doesn't sit well with her either, and by the time she makes it to the restroom, the salivation begins. With the mirror reflecting back the sallowness of her cheeks, Mel spits all the liquid in her mouth, trying to breathe through her nose. Yet the lingering smell of one dump per ten urinations does not, surprisingly, soothe Mel's nausea, pushing it up and out her throat, splashing all over the sink, some of it getting on her clothes.

Giving up hope, Mel makes her way through the shelves of kid's books, board games, laptop bed trays, people moving out of her way in order to avoid the gastric juice odor attached to her. She could easily walk to her manager's office and show him the yellow stains going down her shirt, somewhat of an obvious reason to not stick around. Or if that's unseemly, she could call and say, 'yo, Dan, I just threw up all over myself, see ya some other time'. She much prefers walking on home, dismissing the 805 number that calls an hour later, her weary feet barely making it to the driveway.

Going up the slope nearing an asthma attack, she momentarily draws a blank. What is she doing? She was coming back, yeah, but why? She narrows her eyes confused and steps aside four steps in case that helps her recall. She rubs her temples, stopping in the middle of the driveway, going through her whole day again: woke up, smoked weed, hit the store, went through Artie's shit, had breakfast, was driven to work, read, and then, oh, that's right, the residue in her mouth. She broke into a cold sweat and inevitably vomited. After an arduous search, she seems to have forgotten her Altoids.

Mel is glad to make it home before sundown, the sky a shade of greyish blue escaping the last orange rays behind the purple mountains. The desert envelops the man-made living boxes with its ominous stillness. Tiny rocks crack under Mel's slip resistant shoes, dirt hitting her ankles.

She brashly walks into the middle of a movie Herman and Laura are watching—a P.T. Anderson it seems—and tells them, "I quit my job," before locking herself in her room.

Leaving a crucial scene behind, Herman hardly gives her a beat when he gets up and loudly knocks on her door. She answers with a grunt, opening the door a few seconds later.

"What?" she articulates, her teeth sticky from her accident earlier.

Never giving her the option to explain herself, Herman launches into her room with great force, a savage ire coloring his bald head crimson, the veins on his neck popping out.

"You go on Craigslist and find another job right now!" he roars.

"What the fuck?!" she demands, grabbing her tin of Altoids with trembling hands. "You don't even know—"

"So you're just not gonna have a job?! How easy! You're already not taking your meds and—"

"I'm allergic to it!"

"—now you quit your job?!"

The ridiculousness of her father's frown leading with his cramped bottom teeth, nostrils flaring, snaps like a picture in Mel's mind, burning the pure hatred it temporarily is. Yet as much as Mel understands how transient the argument could be, the thought does not placate her. Weakened by today's events, she erupts herself when she opens the tin of Altoids and it falls open on the floor, littering mints everywhere. At the same time she begins processing this, Herman vigorously grabs her by the wrist, pulling her into twisting her ankle.

"Don't you throw shit!" he yells, the syllables spat at her face.

This is where it starts, where it ends. Before now, everything was still fixable. It could have been a shameful, nasty episode, it could have been forgotten. A lot of fathers have disagreements with their daughters. But when Mel slips out of his grasp, bends, and grabs the Altoids tin, they've both reached the point of no return.

"I didn't throw it! This is throwing it!" and there it goes past Herman's head, hitting the wall.

In one quick movement, Herman gets to Mel's shoulders and shakes her back and forth, her neck limp.

"What's going on?" Laura appears by the door, but this changes nothing. Mel doesn't note it at first, but her face in covered in tears as Herman keeps pushing her around, forcing her to defend herself. She goes for Herman's shirt, ripping off the first two buttons. "Mel!" Laura screams as if it were Mel we should be fearful of.

The girl kicks her way out of her dad's hold, rushing outta there, bumping into Laura whose facial expression shows where she's delivering the blame. The front door lets a gush of air in before closing harshly, resonating off the walls. Good thing she didn't even have the chance to set her purse down, allowing her to flee without having to worry about returning.

"Is she always like this?"

Herman moves his head slightly to make sure he heard her right. "She's always been volatile," he responds, chewing on his finger.

"God...must take after her mother," Laura jokes, as if she knew.

Though he's all for those kinds of comments, it's too soon for Herman. Laura gives him a kiss before he can redirect his anger towards her, leading him back to the living room where the movie's paused.

"There was this one time when she was little—and she's always been very imaginative, creative, artistic, you know, and that combined with her dramatic talents, man, she would make a great actress—so this one time, I think it was her birthday party, we were at my ex's ex's place that year, Mel must have been turning seven or eight...nine...she was making a big fuss about who knows what, big ego thing, something dumb. She had a row with her friends—she was always fighting with someone—and I was obviously trying to just get her to calm down, I mean, the whole family was there, and she kept screaming and whatnot. Crying. And I gave her a chance to talk to me, but she didn't, she wouldn't have it. Then she sort of realized it was time to end it, so she locked herself in the bathroom. Then the problem, as you might have anticipated—"

"How to get her out," Laura interrupts on cue.

"How to get her out, exactly. I left her in there for about an hour, hour and a half—"

"That's a long time for a kid."

"It was enough time to appease her. So when I stopped hearing any sobbing or banging—she would break stuff left and right during her tantrums—I went to the side of the house and climbed in through the window. It was so painful. I think she even laughed at me. I must have looked pathetic. I was a lot chubbier then."

"You? Chubby? Nah."

"Yeah," he nods, standing up, his knees cracking, rasping his way across the carpet to the dining table where Mel left the box of pictures. He looks in there for an appropriate one. "Anyway, the neighbors called the cops and that was another headache.

You wouldn't know how a minor domestic disturbance can be blown up. Look," he says, bringing a photo for Laura to see. She laughs at the decade old image of Herman and Mel at the beach making a sandcastle. He concentrates on the buildings, all a perfect consistency, while Mel works on the moat with twiggy fingers. "See?"

"Raunchy paunchy," Laura taunts, poking Herman's now flat stomach.

But as much as he tries to feel ashamed of his past self, considering how the hair he didn't lose turned gray, wrinkles marking a frown, the inability to sleep and its blue bags, the weight loss doesn't make up for the signs of age, flickering a longing that hadn't been there in a while. He's mostly saddened by Mel's innocent little face, so preoccupied with the task at hand. He taught her his technique so she would eventually win the sandcastle competition with her friends. It was all politics, but at the end of the day, they won.

The Ikea clock reminds him every hour that Mel is still out there. At least she hopes so, sitting on the deck by the leasing office with her feet dangling over the cobweb-ridden bushes below. This wasn't the place she came to first. After running out, she kept on going, out of the complex and onto the dark street only visible in the headlights of passing cars. At the gas station, she broke the hundred her mother gave her in case of an emergency by buying a Red Bull, some Starbursts, and a pack of Camel Crushes. She's been chain-smoking since then, about to run out of matches what with most of them not working.

A Prius makes its silent way up the driveway. Mel catches a glimpse of it but overlooks it thinking it's just another flash in the corner of her eye. It's as if they happen more in the dark when it's most disorienting. Trying to stay away from hypochondria, she hasn't Googled what it could be. She figures it must have to do with her right eye again, its astigmatism or whatever, even if the left also fucks up. In anthropology class her first semester of college, she learned that an embryo divides in half when it comes to developing the left and right sides of the body. Someone with perfect symmetry therefore becomes a great specimen in contrast to those whose left side doesn't exactly match up with the right. A tumultuous pregnancy is at fault. Or maybe that's wrong, Mel can't remember. She had a hard time concentrating and she never studied, just winged it. However, that would explain why her nose is crooked, why more hair grows in one armpit than the other, why her eyes can't be on the same page.

can i stay at your place tonight?

Half an hour goes by, more cars arrive home, passersby walk their dogs sensing a presence in the foliage. Mel takes the first drag of a new cigarette, savoring the tobacco before crushing it. *The Hurting* plays softly through her shitty cell phone speaker.

sure. i'll be there around eleven thirty. is everything okay?

Putting his cell phone away before getting caught, Jameson starts to wonder what kind of night he's in for. Is she gonna joke around, mope around, jump his bones, jump down his throat, it could be anything. The only sure thing is his will to stay patient.

He brings dessert to one of his tables. When it looks like they're done, they ask for more strawberries. Since they've been drinking and eating for two hours, Jameson brings them a bunch for free. They tip twenty percent.

The Cavalier doesn't once turn on. The way it sounded earlier when he went up Lakeview Canyon Road warned him it could happen again tonight. He runs back into the restaurant to see if anyone can give him a ride, but the coworkers left are douches. He'd rather walk. The car can wait till tomorrow.

car gave up. walking home.

Goddammit, goes Mel's stomach. She's been sitting here for hours thinking all the gruesome thoughts that come with being forsaken: torture, rape, murder.

get an uber or a lyft or whatever. i'll pay for it.

ha, in this town? chill. it won't take that long.

Yes, yes it will take that long. She starts typing a text detailing what happened so he'd do as she says, but upon reading it, she deletes all of it, putting the cell phone down, the music struggling to play with a dozen other apps open.

She waits. Just fucking waits.

Artie's real name is Matilda Bonham. Pollo must be Samuel Bonham. Tilly and Sam.

She goes on IMDb. No Matilda Bonham. Or Artemis Waltz.

Mel knocks on her head in case that makes it work. The five Ws, her eyes going blind, the feeling of dread, all at once overwhelming her.

She's got her suspicions but she's wary about facing them. The more she thinks about it, the more her head hurts, among other symptoms. And the less she thinks about it, well, that's not an option. Bending her neck, Mel looks up at the sky where the shadow of an imaginary palm tree appears and disappears as she blinks.

Vinnie Beck. A thorough search of news articles indicate his car rolled off Mulholland Drive into a famous person's house at five in the morning while he was under the influence of a substance or other, none of which is mentioned by his friends and family on the Facebook page, full of life this, always remembered that. No murder mystery here.

A lifetime later, Jameson can be seen panting his way up the driveway. Mel's first instinct is to shout his name, but another flash prevents her from doing so, her voice getting stuck at the uvula. The volume on her phone lowers to emit the beep of a new text message: *getting home now.*

There's no need to respond. She simply stands up, brushes the dead leaves off her butt, and follows Jameson. He doesn't notice her at all, entering his apartment just to be interrupted by Mel's knocking thirty seconds later. Standing in the faint light of the landing, she looks beautiful. He wants to tell her this without making her uncomfortable, so he doesn't say anything.

Already turning around to head back in, Jameson doesn't see it coming when, out of a deep need, Mel wraps her arms all the way around him from behind, clasping her hands at the front. Taken aback by her suddenness, he stands still while she squeezes him.

"Thank you," she whispers.

"For what?"

He feels her shrug her shoulders, and as soon as she's about to pull away, he takes hold of her and tightens the embrace. Feeling bold, he turns his head and kisses her somewhere on the face. Remarkably, she kisses him back. Her lips are chapped, her nose cold, her taste revealing just how many cigarettes she managed to smoke in the last five hours. They make out all the way to the bedroom where Mel tries to get Jameson on the inflatable mattress.

"I really need to shower first," he insists as Mel starts to unbutton his shirt.

"It's okay."

"No, really."

"I've been waiting forever."

Smiling to repress a laugh, Jameson undoes the hug. "Quick shower. Promise. You can play GTA meanwhile."

She nods, turning on the Xbox. The water runs as Mel, in her own words, nills some kiggas. Jameson's quick shower takes about forty minutes, coming out wrapped in a striped pink towel. A tad shy about it, he removes it and proceeds to get dressed. Mel tries not to look—tunnel vision video game playing—but just like the flashes and shadows, she cannot ignore his presence in the corner of her eye. She thought leaving a toothbrush in his bathroom was the strongest way of accepting their newfound commitment, but clearly there's room for more.

"So what happened? You look pretty upset."

"I thought you were just gonna leave it at pretty."

"That too," he gets away with saying.

"I don't really remember anymore," Mel admits. "My dad got super mad at me and it got kinda violent so I left. No, wait, actually, lemme start again. I basically quit my job by not showing up. Who the fuck cares?! I'm earning minimum wage serving food at a dine-in movie theater. You'd think, oh, well, there's gotta be tips in that. Nope. Too busy watching the movie, the fucking fuckers!"

"You'll find something better."

"Who even wants that kind of service while they're watching a film anyway? It's so distracting! But that's not the point. The point's that he's a goddamn egotistical prick, annoyed he has to spend money on me, oh no! Why the fuck have a child if you don't wanna actually have a child?"

"Maybe it's 'cause you're older now."

"Twenty-one, eight, makes no difference. Once when I was little I asked him if he could buy me an ice cream, and you know what he said? He said that's what he gave my mom child support for."

"So you didn't get an ice cream."

"Not once."

"What an asshole."

"Tell me about it."

"Why on Earth did you move in with him?"

"To leave my mother in peace, I dunno. Give myself time to think."

"Is it working?"

"Well," she murmurs, her eyes getting lost inside her head with the flashes and shadows. "Wait, what were we talking about?"

"Your dad?"

"Oh."

"Are you okay?"

"Yeah, I just—I don't fucking know, man. Must be all that wax we've been smoking. Got me all forgetful and shit."

Fully dressed now, Jameson pats her on the upper arm. She raises it to her cheek.

"Are you hungry?" he asks.

"I can be."

They smoke a few bowls and Jameson makes spaghetti with cheese-filled meatballs just so they can go smoke some more when they're done eating. If it's not to get an appetite, it's to alleviate the fullness of a meal.

In efforts to get her in the mood again—he didn't want to take advantage of her distress earlier—Jameson lights some candles in his room, leaving the Christmas lights on around the window. They cuddle on the inflatable mattress under a few blankets. Jameson smells like soap, his spiky stubble prickling Mel wherever he kisses her. She doesn't react well, her eyes wide and focused on the wall.

"Do you think I have daddy issues?" she whimpers with a giggle.

"Well, are you a slut?"

"You know, I hate how cliché my life's turned out. We used to get along when I was little, me, Mom and Dad. Then the divorce came and poof. I mean, he probably thinks he loves me a lot, but he wouldn't even pick me up from Riverside. Shit like that. My mom offered to drive me, but I'm tired of making her do everything."

"Do you get along with her better?"

"Yeah, she cares. She's aware. We fight a lot, but, like, it's fine, I guess. She's not very affectionate, but she's always made sure I have everything. My dad's very huggy-kissy, cries of joy and stuff, but he won't even buy me an ice cream or give me a ride or anything. Any time I've ever complained about his fatherly duties, he shuts me up by saying I'm just saying what my mom says, making shit up and taking it all against him. Clearly he was projecting, but you don't get that at that age. And that's been my relationship with him since I was six. You're very lucky, you know?"

"I'm probably the only person I know whose parents are still together."

"And you have a bunch of siblings too. An actual family. I got the bastardized version." He laughs, kissing her again. She avoids his mouth. "You're such a pest!"

"I'm just giving you kisses."

"I can see that. Sorry, I just—I've told you I'm not too touchy-feely."

They fall into an awkward silence. The candles flicker, tumbling Mel's vision. The contrast between light and dark plays with her thoughts. She looks at Jameson without being able to explain herself.

"Can I have half a Seroquel? I kinda just wanna sleep through all this bullshit," she begs.

Happy to be of help, Jameson gets up and retrieves a Target medicine bottle from the closet. He breaks the pill in half and gives her the smaller piece, taking the bigger one for himself along with a Mirtazapine. There's a ten-minute window before he passes out cold.

The Christmas lights are unplugged early tonight, but the candlewicks keep burning, leaving a scent composed of vanilla, fresh linens, and Skittles—the things you find at Dollar Tree sometimes. Mel's eyelids begin to get lazy. It starts as a blessing, Jameson's willingness to share his medication with her more than she could ever ask for, but as soon as he's dormant, being alone sparks that feeling of dread, the penumbra on the walls forming into smothering silhouettes. She draws the covers over her face. The tiny child self crawls back out of the past, and all Mel can do is snivel, trying not to wake up Jameson.

9

The hollow click of the front door shutting makes Mel sit up, the harsh sunlight hitting her in the face. Out of breath, she looks at the sleeping Jameson by her side. He's unconsciously scratching the hairy part of his chest, his eyes moving rapidly under the spell of a dream. It reminds her of what she was dreaming. It wasn't a regular night mara. Something else happened.

"Fuck," she mutters to herself.

It's too late now. All she's left with is the image of going down a street overlooked by palm trees, the sun at its highest. By the time she's ready to go use the bathroom, the dream is completely gone.

"Oh," says a voice from the kitchen.

Mel rubs her eyes clean in order to look at Artie's face, her glasses left behind in the bedroom. "Hey," she goes.

"Hi."

The five foot two, twenty-four-year-old suspect stands with one hand on her waist, the other bent with a large purse hanging from the elbow. Her bleached hair is a mess, like if she had braided it and then brushed through the braids, breaking it to stick out in all directions. In toe socks and flip-flops paired with baggy sweatpants and a wrinkled Lana Del Rey T-shirt, she doesn't appear so glamorous. But besides a little bit of blood residue under one of her nostrils, she seems to be all right. The Chihuahua prances around glad to be home.

"Dope shirt."

"Thanks." And then before Mel can take a piss: "So you're fucking now?"

The question, meant to shock, doesn't move Mel at all. She stares Artie down. The dark roots, the gaunt cheekbones, yesterday's lipstick painting the portrait of a hot mess.

Out of nervousness, it seems, Artie reaches into her purse and retrieves her Kiss Superslims, lighting one with a golden zippo.

"Can I have one of those?" Mel asks in response to Artie's daring demeanor.

"Sure…"

Distrustful, Artie hands her one. When Mel puts it between her parched lips, Artie goes ahead and—after a few tries with those asparagus fingers—lights it for her. Interesting flavor. They stay like that for a few drags, both of them waiting for the other one to make the next move.

And then, with a rush of adrenaline: "Who are you?"

"Excuse me?"

Artie takes a step backward, but Mel makes up for it by taking one forward. The height difference leads Artie to hold her head high, quick to twiddle with her pendant. Mel's stomach churns. Artie hears it.

"Yeah, who are you?"

Artie's mouth curves upward, but it's not pleasant. Those transparent black blue eyes covered in chunky mascara don't disengage Mel's, even when this one looks away intimidated. Otherwise keeping it cool, Artie readjusts the elastic band of her sweats at the hipbone. A small bulge around the belly-button area shows the signs of a ring. She's one of those girls, the ones who tan before going to the beach, buy outfits strictly for Coachella, and occasionally treat themselves to a session of chew and spit.

"Who am I?" Cigarette smoke escapes Artie's mouth with a pack of lies. "I don't know. Who am I?"

"Tilly," Mel accuses before turning the knob on the bathroom door, Artie freezing in position, ash getting on the carpet.

The throbbing headache that follows sends Mel to the toilet just so she can sit down, first of all, her blood pressure dropping. What is it with these fucking people? They're on to us, they're on to us, they must be thinking. The problems with Mel's vision return, and shorty after she's regained her balance, a panic attack hits her. She presses against her chest, slightly assuaging the hyperventilation. Tilly and Sam, Tilly and Sam.

The palm tree shadows make her dizzy. She pushes her middle fingers to her temples, a vacuous humming in her ears, her left boob pumping to the accelerated heartbeat. With great difficulty, Mel stands up to dampen her face, only a head rush collapses her, the rug underneath her feet still moist from Jameson's shower in the unventilated room slipping, tripping her onto the sink counter face first.

10

Fifteen seconds go by in black as Mel hears her uneven breathing and nothing else, counting down to open her eyes. A trickling leaves the left one purblind as the walls wobble diagonally, imitating the nausea. She pulls herself up heftier than usual and looks in the mirror: her brow is gashed open. It bleeds down the side of her face all the way down her neck without coagulating, past her collarbone, her breast, draining her.

11

Palm trees rise above, sending Mel down the road to the beach where Tilly holds her by the hand as Sam takes the lead, running towards the ocean. There's a common elatedness as the sun shines over the hot sand and cold water. Tilly looks back at Mel with a grin, her full light brown hair in a sturdy ponytail decorated with a silk red ribbon tied in a loose bow that keeps getting blown on her face.

"We won!" Tilly shouts. "We won!"

Her feet catch on somebody's towel and she slips momentarily before Mel can catch her at the last second, both of them laughing their way back up.

"Come on, loser," Mel kids, resuming their race.

Behind them, taking their time, Herman, Carine, and Mr. and Mrs. Bonham walk proud of their children. They have no reason to be but can't help it.

Out of breath, Mel slows down, losing the twins. Her chest belabors and her head goes light, suddenly beaten against the hard ground, sweated on, spat at, nervous laughter coming from a corner inciting on.

"Night Mara! Night Mara!" they chant as the punches keep coming. More feet, more fists. Pounding and pounding and pounding. "No, no," they say as, through blood and loose eyelashes, Mel watches Mara wipe her hands on her flannel shirt, her eyelid twitching. "You gotta do it like this."

Mel's head falls with a bad crackling sound, throwing stars into her field of view. She coughs and the pain takes her further into the blinking white, the surrounding black, the promise that this, too, shall pass, perhaps and hopefully forever.

12

"Mel, please, are you all right in there?" Jameson keeps trying to open the door, but it's locked. He knocks a bunch of times. "Mel!"

The walls whiten, the light sharpens, and one exhalation behind, Mel begins to appreciate what just happened. She rises to her feet, opening the door.

"Hey—"

"Mel!" he gasps. "What the fuck?!"

Artie's standing in the living room trying not to pry. When Mel makes eye contact with her, she slides into her bedroom, letting them know that: "I won't put up with this shit!"

"It's cool," Mel says about her cut when he inspects it, tenderly turning her head by the chin.

"No, no, dude, you might need stitches. Just look at this thing!"

"It's fine. I—"

"You were in there for forty minutes! What happened? What were you—are you all right?"

"Yeah, I just...fuck!" The wound leaks into her eye. She takes the bottom of her Flogging Molly T-shirt and wipes her face with it, ruining it permanently. "Forty minutes?"

"Yeah, Artie kept waiting around to take a shower, and you never answered when she knocked, so she woke me up." It sounds like a grouse. "You should go to urgent care or something."

Shaking her head, Mel gets her keys from her shelf in Jameson's closet.

"I'll be right back," she tells him before stepping out of the apartment, only plaguing him some more.

Having stood by the bathroom hollering and trying to force the door open, by now all Jameson can think of is finally taking a leak himself. Towel in hand, Artie makes her way to the bathroom to find it locked again.

"Fuck you, dude!"

Very aware that when she needs to shower, she needs to shower, he takes his time.

After checking the garage to make sure the Malibu's gone, Mel sneaks into Herman's apartment to gather a few things. Since it's Saturday, she has no idea where he could have gone, when he could return. She hurries out and comes back to Jameson's only to find the front door locked. She knocks a few times and a few times more. Artie must have locked her out. Mel's cell phone is in Jameson's room. Fuck, fuck, fuck.

And just when things can't get any shittier, a gut feeling makes her glance down the driveway as the Malibu enters the garage. Out of pure desperation, she knocks, slaps, jabs Jameson's window. She does the same to the front door, kicks it even. Artie, have some mercy! Please, please, please.

Half a minute passes before the blinds on Jameson's window part at the middle. He sees Mel put her hands together, palm to palm in prayer. He identifies her exigency and lets her in right away so she may wait by the peephole. Sure enough, Herman and Laura go up the stairs carrying boxes. She must be moving in.

"I'm really sorry about that. It's just that...look," she says to Jameson when they get to his bedroom, dropping her backpack and laptop case on the floor. "Something...something happened...a long time ago...Artie..." Not meaning to leave him hanging, Mel rolls her tongue around, too shaken up to talk. The lively color in her face is gone, the circles under her eyes stamped like hematomas, and since she doesn't want to sound out of it, her features contort into cartoonish faces. "I had a flashback in the bathroom after I slip—"

"A flashback?"

"Yeah, I mean, I don't know what else to call it. Shit. I fucking traveled through time, dude! It was...it was fucked up."

Distressed by the melodrama, Jameson holds his hands before him, expecting a more relieving answer, some reassuring explanations.

"Are you all right?" he asks for the third time.

"Yeah, but it's...fuck...it's fucked up...this's never happened to me before...I...I could smell the ocean, taste the blood," she keeps working through the words, chewing on her cheek, gathering her thoughts as fast as she can. "Great defense mechanism, forgetting. Starts to falter with time, it seems. Like becoming an adult wasn't already hard enough. It gets to a point where you fucking birth it outta the hells of your subconscious right into your eyeballs, goddammit, just in case you're the absentminded type!" She picks at a pimple on her chin. "It's like, I get it, psyche! Night Mara, Artie, everything! I was wondering why, but I needn't worry about why. What about it? That's what I'm trying to get at, right? So what? Mara beat me up. Who cares? What's the point? And what about Tilly, I mean, I..."

He wants to say something but can't come up with anything appropriate or original. Instead, he nods sympathetically, his mouth pouting somewhat.

Mel stares into the distance focusing on nothing but the shadows on the wall. Perhaps she shouldn't have told Jameson. He's gonna think she's too much. Nonetheless, she nods, getting ready to vent the rest, popping her daily Wellbutrin.

"I was—I was running with Tilly and Sam...at the beach...we were all really happy...and then...aah! It just hurts so much," and she puts her hand to her eyes, covering up her ugly crying. "God! I just can't fucking...argh!" Jameson puts his hand on her shoulder, but the gesture startles Mel, who jerks away from him as if ready to attack. "No, don't."

"Sorry," he says sincerely.

With her mouth open, totally absorbed by the visions, Mel doesn't hear his apology. He watches her connecting strings, tying them around loose thumbtacks.

"It's...it's..." she says to herself. "Yeah, I mean, yeah, of course."

"What?"

"I guess...this is just so..." She covers her face in shame. "So you know how time is like a staircase?"

"If you say so, sure."

"Well, to me it is. You give me a date and I feel it on the staircase, and the steps are the color of the days—never mind, whatever. It's just like...when I get really depressed, my mind fucks up. Sometimes I can't handle things, so recalling those moments is super hard 'cause the memories are dimly lit. My life literally drains of color. Just like good times are so vibrant."

"I feel you."

"But there's this...period...summer...when I turned eight. It— it was completely black. I didn't notice until recently. And then I met her. Heaven-sent chance!" she attempts to laugh.

"Jesus, you're not okay. You're still shaking."

"I am?" Mel looks at her hands. He's right. "I feel like someone reached into my brain and rewired me all wrong."

"Yeah, you're smelling apparitions and going up and down time."

"Minor case of synesthesia. Might have done too much acid."

"Mel, please, your eyebrow—"

"It's fine," she groans more sexually than painfully. "I'll ask my dad to take me to the doctor."

"You sure?"

"Yeah, I'm not gonna, like, go to the ER."

"This is exactly what the ER is for."

"And it also costs like a thousand dollars. Or I have the worst insurance."

Mel goes to the kitchen and takes a paper towel, folds it in eighths, and flattens it on the wet hack. The white rapidly turns red. Jameson predicts negligence will get the best of her. Still under the influence of his meds, the return to normal makes him sleepy again. He tries to stay awake to hear Mel sigh every few seconds as if asking to be asked what fucked up shit she's thinking. Eventually the disquiet becomes contagious and Jameson rubs his eyes, cleaning them out to leave them open. He cracks his back, then his knuckles, chuckling every time Mel flinches.

"What time is it?"

She checks her watch on the floor. "Twelve fifteen."

"Oh," he yawns.

He takes Mel's hand, and they cuddle for a long while talking about everything lighthearted they can think of to keep themselves distracted.

"Nick Mason's—I like him and everything—but, I dunno, he's a real perfectionist. I prefer Mitch Mitchell. John Bonham," he says, doing exactly what they were trying not to do.

A few bowls later, Jameson makes breakfast as he gets dressed. All ready to go, he sits with Mel to enjoy the meal. She finishes everything on her plate like she does, he leaves a little behind like he does. He insists she stay while he's away at work if she wants to. She takes him up for it. He rolls his bike out of the balcony and puts a flashlight in his backpack, the Cavalier still stuck in the restaurant's parking lot. After kissing her goodbye, he's possessed by an insatiable need to come back home already. His work suffers. It gets pretty busy and everyone starts acting like a dick. Cody chats up a girl at the bar instead of making drinks, Riley has some youngsters dine dash on him, and Mandy gets caught secretly adding 18% to all parties of six or more without telling them to receive another tip. Those are the highlights. His aptitude going unappreciated, Jameson starts to near a hundred dollars in tips halfway through his shift.

everything good? he texts Mel.

yeah, just took a nap.

She paces in his bedroom after having lain in bed for a while with her eyes closed. Her problems got more strident, so at a certain point it became impaling to remain so, getting up to pick a record. *Surfer Rosa* plays as Mel finds a comfortable spot on the inflatable mattress, all the blankets bunched up under and around her. The songs remind her of sexual abuse, insanity, the beach. Figurative figures dance from white to black with panting breaths.

Frustrated, Mel digs into her giant purse and extracts the purple pen alongside a gas station receipt.

- *Fall 1999, 6: Divorce*
- *Summer 2000, 7: Birthday with Dad (Thousand Oaks)*
- *Summer 2001, 8: ?*
- *Summer 2002, 9: Birthday with Mom (Riverside)*

Carine's old house, the Polaroid camera, Tilly and Sam and I win, Wes shows me *The Texas Chain Saw Massacre*, Mara beats me up. The thoughts race entering a more manic mood.

Now that this is happening, Mel...well, she thinks she's lost it. Yet it comes with the suspicion that she's making shit up to convince herself she's gone insane, therefore destroying herself some more, rendering her capable of less and less responsibilities. That! That must be her desire! She touches the cut on her brow, fingers returning as red as Tilly's ribbon. If only she could talk to her.

After debating it for a while, Mel comes out of her hiding spot to encounter an empty living room, Artie's door closed. Relieved, she leaves, the key Jameson left her in her pocket.

Bold and relatively flippant, Mel lets herself into her father's apartment. First she finds Laura sitting on the couch watching TV surrounded by bags and boxes. Neither of the women says anything. This gives Mel permission to walk further inside. Herman is in the kitchen with his back to them cooking something on the stove. He doesn't turn around. Mel keeps making her way to her bedroom and no one stops her.

She thinks she'll pick up more things to bring over to Jameson's, but the urge to wreak havoc is stronger than her will. Stomping with her Converse, each bend eating away the tearing fabric, Mel goes back to the living room and opens the box of pictures on the dining table. She feels Herman's eyes at the back of her neck, fingers flicking through the photos fast, fixated on finding the image she's looking for. And there it is, the one of Mel ripping apart gift wrap while Herman flips burgers.

"When was this?" she demands of her seemingly sulky father who dismissively looks at what she's holding up, keeping his mouth shut for as long as he can. "Mh?"

"Your birthday...at Carine's," he breaks, as if mentioning the name was improper in Laura's presence.

"What happened?"

Herman doesn't look at her like someone who's free of sin. Perhaps aware of what she's referring to, perhaps not, he doesn't let anything slip.

"What happened is you were spoiled and made a fuss about everything," he tells her maliciously. "You stole from Carine to buy you and your friends ice cream, and you kept calling your mom any time I nagged you, and she was on my ass about every little thing you told her."

"No, that's not what I mean."

"What do you mean then?!"

He lays his fist forcefully on the cutting board, a significant amount of diced bell peppers falling on the floor.

"Mara beat me up. Remember?! Fucked me up pretty good. That's why my mom was on your ass."

"No," he grunts. "Your mom was calling to make sure you wore sunblock. That kind of thing. And your stepsister did that to you because you got her in trouble. You weren't a sweet, little innocent kid, Mel. You were unbearable!"

"That's not what I'm interested in."

"What do you want?!"

"I want the truth!"

With her index finger pointed in no particular direction, tongue licking the bottom of her upper teeth, thighs slipping to the edge of the seat, Laura gets ready to interrupt: "Was that when the cops showed up because you locked yourself in the bathroom?"

Both Mel and Herman look at her like she's crossed a line, but Laura is immune to their despicable game. Yet the reminder allows Mel to place the episode on her timeline, a raving vehemence released by her brain's intermittent chemistry.

"Yeah!" Mel yells, light bulbs glimmering. "That was when I ran from all of you by going to the bathroom, and before I could lock myself in, you pushed it all the way in and hit me on the head with the fucking huge-ass wooden door. And then I closed it on your fingers and that's when you left me be. My head immediately swelled up and it hurt so much I was crying—"

"You were already crying!"

"That's because something happened! What happened?!"

"Mel," says Laura, asking her to stop.

Maintaining eye contact with Herman, Mel gives up before things get a chance to escalate. She promptly puts into effect Laura's order, going to her room to gather her valuables. She sticks them in one of her suitcases with haste, the clothes taking up much more room than if they were folded neatly.

"You need to calm down!" Herman bellows, suddenly walking in, kicking some shirts out of his path.

"I did. Maybe you should too," Mel responds softly to contrast his tone.

"You listen to me! I'm your father!"

"What the fuck does that even mean?" she scoffs. "It's not that hard to become a father. I hear it's a quite pleasurable experience actually. But being a father, well, that's a whole different story you've never written and I've never read!"

"You think you're so clever!" With that frown, the cramped bottom teeth showing in the rhythm of his flaring nostrils, he kicks more clothes out of the way and gets to Mel. "You get out of this house! Get out!" he roars satanically, raising his fist.

"Hit me! Come on, if you wanna hit me, then fucking hit me!" she dares him, standing two inches taller than him.

Unlike what she thought would happen, Herman flattens out his hand and smacks her left cheek with enough force to leave a red print all over that side of her face. He grabs her by the shoulders and begins to shake her, only this time Mel's prepared. She wiggles out of his grip and quickly socks him in the throat, then ducks under his hands and lands by the suitcase.

"Get out!" he goes one more time, kicking more clothes.

Mel tries to fight back tears, but she can't afford that kind of concentration right now. Soon her face is all wet, the suitcase almost ready, if only Herman would stop messing with her things. He keeps going on and on about her leaving faster, but Mel blocks it out by screaming in her head. Against Mel's insistence that the other key on her chain isn't for his apartment, he takes both keys from her by forcefully digging into her pocket. She frees herself once more, zips the suitcase in one swooping motion—unable to finish packing, the records left behind—and runs out of Herman's chase. Laura has not moved, sitting there shaking her head.

"Get out, Mel," she says. "Now."

Finding humor in it, Mel drags her suitcase through everything it comes across, leaving a trail of cables and magazines and shoes. The landing feels cool once Herman bangs the door shut. If she stays outside any longer, it'll get chilly. It took a long time to get to this point this year. Must be climate change.

Starting to fret, Mel walks with her suitcase rolling off on its side due to the uneven weight of it. Dammit, she realizes with one interrupted step. She forgot her bag of socks.

It doesn't even take a minute to make it to Jameson's. The light is on. It could only mean one thing. This being her only chance, she knocks.

"It's Mel," she tells the other side.

"Well, hello," Artie greets her perkily as if enjoying seeing Mel like this.

"Sorry. I kind of just got kicked out of my house," she explains.

"Fucky."

"Yeah."

Artie moves aside to let her in—a gesture Mel was unsure would happen—then locks the door twice, peeking out of the peephole before turning to Mel. They both sit on the couch's armrests.

"Is Jameson at work?" Mel nods. "He says you saw my brother around," she lays on Mel, trying to hide her importunity.

"When you weren't here, yeah. I thought he might be looking for you."

"We got into a fight so I wasn't speaking to him," Artie articulates through the cigarette propped between her lips. "How do you know my brother?"

Venom swirls through the room. Mel can almost see it when the corners of her eyes flash. She swallows, trying to breathe through her mouth. The walls close in, the Kramer poster and the DVD shelf with Artie's Criterion Collections, Jameson's *Scarface*, his *Godfather II*...

"I'm not sure," Mel admits, reaching for the cigarette Artie's offering, sweat starting to build up around her hairline. "Or you but—but I do." As lightly as possible, Artie chews on the inside of her lip, her pretense fading. "I'm gonna be totally honest with you." Mel lights the cigarette, lets out a big puff of smoke, and reaches into her back pocket. "But you have to be totally honest with me." Mel stares into her eyes, disappointed with their lack of commitment. But now it's much too late to shut up. "When I met you I felt like I knew you...but I don't, and it's—it's—" she lets out with febrile tears forming in her bloodshot eyes. "It's dri—dri—driving me—"

"Chill! Chill!" Artie cuts in, jumping to her bare feet, red polish chipping off her toenails. "Please chill! Just—ugh!" she adds, blenching, burying her face in her hands.

Weirded out, Mel halts all emotion one drag after another, watching Artie's blond hair sway from side to side around her bent head. In this light, Artie isn't at all someone to fear. The defeated girl forgets about the ash building on her cigarette and so it falls to the floor. Tiny wrists rotate cracking as she doesn't attempt to get herself together.

"Look, I've this..." Mel murmurs, finally taking a chance, regretting it already, unveiling the Polaroid. She's not too sure of what she's doing, Artie's reaction with no basis for prediction. The thing is there's nothing else left to do.

Artie eyes the Polaroid through her fingers as if she already knows what it is.

"You can't tell anyone."

Mel's heart pumps twice as many times as it's supposed to. Finally after all this misery! She tightens the grip around her cigarette as it begins to burn the filter.

"Tell anyone what?" she whispers dryly, getting it across mildly.

"Look at me," Artie says as if it were obvious.

"What? What happened?"

Artie crosses her arms, incapable of saying the words out loud. "I—I," she stutters. "I used to be fat." Her eyes rolling back, Mel bends at the ankle and stumbles sideways. "Oh my god!" A skinny arm helps her back on the sofa. She slides voluntarily and lands on the middle cushion. "Are you anemic or something?"

"I just might be," Mel responds with a bubble in her throat. "But no, that's not—that's not—" she maintains, but Artie keeps staring right through her, sternly waiting for a confirmation that her secret will not be revealed. "Why all the theatrics? Changing your name, that's not something every person who loses weight does. Did you," she lets slip before she can think about what she's saying, "did you get surgery?"

Underneath her long strawy tresses, Artie sniffles. She's got a pointy little nose and sharp chin, her upper lip an upside down copy of the bottom one. Her eyes are a black shade of blue, off, totally off, just like her amity doesn't deliver. Unknown to her what Artie's deal is, Mel keeps wondering what makes her so undesirable. In essence she's a pretty girl, sounds like she could be kinda funny, but there's something rotten about her.

"Ugh, here's the deal...I don't even know why I'm doing this," Artie takes an aside. "All right, so...before we 'went to college abroad,'" she admits using air quotes, "there was a lot going on. I was eighteen, my father died, and I was also seeing this guy, hanging out with this crowd, and then...anyway, I received threats," she spits with a slither, "so I thought it would be smart to start over, reenter life as a comely, healthy girl. Besides there was nothing to be proud of. I'd achieved nothing as of then. I did what I had to do and voilà. You can imagine everything was oh so perfect. The problem's too many people know me around here. It's not so easy acting like I don't know them. But imagine if they found out."

"Who cares? You're beautiful."

"I care."

"But what about your family?" Mel asks enthralled.

"Yeah, sure, they weigh me down a bit, but certain ties just can't...you just can't, you know?"

"So they're all aware."

"No one's gonna betray me. Not a peep."

"But there's gotta be—I mean, family friends, neighbors, what—what—"

"I never said it was a good plan. In fact, I almost wish I hadn't gone through with it," and a tear escapes her eye. "But I had to do it," she reassures herself. "I had to."

"I'm—I'm sorry," Mel struggles to say, doubting she'll ever hear the whole story. "You didn't have to tell me all this."

"Yes, I did. You don't know how you looked a couple of minutes ago. Half-mad. But it's not like I haven't had to come clean before," she adds full of rue.

"I thought it was a lot more serious," Mel drops, trying to trap her.

Artie straightens up, lighting another cigarette. "How do you mean?" She offers one to her new confidante but she shakes her head.

"I'm all nicotined out," Mel says before changing her mind. "Actually, yeah, thanks. I just thought—look, you don't even know. Long story short, I've been thinking a lot about that summer and, man, I...I just don't remember it, just bits here and there. That's why I'm all, like, suspicious, I guess. But what about your brother?"

"What about him?"

"Why did he change his name? Just for consistency?"

"He's my twin brother," Artie fails to explain since it's all she knows. "If I'm gonna be Artie, he's gonna be Pollo."

"But doesn't that...I mean, liposuction...why the face?" Mel keeps wondering when nothing adds up. "You weren't ugly."

"Thanks, but it's complicated. I don't expect you to understand."

"You're an artist, right?"

"Yeah," Artie answers superficially.

"I imagine there's a lot of pressure about your appearance in your field?"

"You don't even know. And I used to want to be an actress. But I'm done with that life," Artie appends, sliding her ruby pendant up and down the white gold chain.

"So wait, then why did you—"

"Like I said!" Artie emphasizes, raising her voice. "It's complicated. But hey, what matters is that you're not going nuts, right?" she babbles on speedily.

"Right," Mel murmurs unsure. "I do know you."

"You do." Artie smiles her pearly white teeth to rush her way out of the uncomfortable conversation. "Hey, do you want me to take a look at that cut? I'm a pretty good nurse."

With the calid tone in which she says it, changing into a different person completely, Artie awakens another side of Mel.

"Um, okay."

Holding her cigarette in one hand, Artie goes through the medicine cabinet. She returns to the living room with a couple of cotton balls, peroxide, Neosporin, gauze, and tape. Blowing smoke in Mel's face, she works on the inch-long wound, giving the convalescent the good kind of sting.

"I love taking care of people," Artie says, but Mel has trouble deciding whether it's honest.

They remain there for a while as Artie wraps up, having another cigarette each. Artie hums "Happiness Is a Warm Gun," then apologizes for being annoying, telling Mel it's been stuck in her head all day. She doesn't know why. Just woke up like that. Mel says that happens to her every day. When she's done speaking, she shivers uncontrollably, causing Artie to giggle and ask if she's cold. No, not at all, Mel evokes with a shake of the head and too much blinking. She just needs the bathroom. Excuse her.

Making it, though barely, Mel sits on the toilet unable to see anymore, her oily hair on her face the only thing not moving. Too many, just too many cigarettes.

She flushes the toilet to keep it real, then washes her face and hands. When she comes across her own face in the mirror, it takes her a while to recognize herself. It's the first time she sees how old she's grown. She'll never be this young again. Shake it off. Breathe.

Her return to the living room is expected by an agitated Artie who seems to have something important to say, but instead of spitting it out already, she waits for Mel to ask.

"Yes?" she finally does.

"You look awful—"

"Thanks—"

"How about we go out to dinner?" Cheerfully, Artie waits for Mel to catch up. "On me."

"I, uh," Mel mumbles. "Sure, yeah."

"Perfect."

Dutifully, the younger lass follows the smaller one—Chihuahua in hand—to a black convertible Mini Cooper full of fast food bags. Embarrassed, Artie sticks them under the seats. "Pollo," she blames.

Artie keeps the ride silent. She smokes another cigarette on the 101 as Mel looks out the window, crossing into the San Fernando Valley. Traffic builds up and Artie takes out her cell phone to make a call. While she waits to be answered, she gussies up on the visor mirror by licking her lips, duck-facing as if looking more presentable could sway the other end.

"Come on, Cassie, don't be a bitch. I'm offering you a hundred fucking dollars." Artie swerves, avoiding the 405. "'Kay," she lets out relieved. "I'll be there soon."

It takes them a while to get to Burbank, an accident on the 134 leaving it at a standstill. They hit up a Bank of America ATM and Artie takes out two hundred dollars. She counts the bills before dividing the stack of twenties, half for her wallet, the other in her bra. A stoned punk girl meets them outside her house and gives them six bars of Xanax in exchange for the cash in Artie's shirt as Celeste barks uncontrollably. Cassie tells Artie about a Sex Stains show she couldn't get into. Man, that sucks. The girl waves goodbye and leaves, never acknowledging Mel.

"Here," Artie shuffles, turning on the light. "Take some. We'll save the rest for later."

Mel gladly takes them from the open hand, chugging half a water bottle that Artie offers her right after. Artie takes a tiny gulp herself after getting rid of a couple of pills. They buy more cigarettes at an obscure cigar shop not far from there, and by the time they get to Ventura Boulevard—the constructions on Magnolia/Whitsett and Moorpark/Coldwater Canyon delaying them somewhat—Mel starts relaxing.

"It's gonna be three instead, if that's all right," Mel hears Artie tell someone while being lead down an unfamiliar setting, Celeste still in her arm.

"Not a problem," says a semi-welcoming, semi-disgusted, and also, my god, semi-afraid female voice.

She invites them into a little room with draped curtains and romantic lighting where a gentleman, so tall he looks awkward on the low sofa, lounges in a corner. Saying something about the dog not being allowed there, Pollo waves her away with a large bill.

"Pollo, this is Mel," Artie reintroduces them.

"Yeah," says Pollo. "Hi."

"See? He remembers me," Mel jokes lazily.

"It's cool. I told her." Artie chimes in.

"About your reconstruction?" Artie stares at the ground offended, the acerbic tone perhaps unappreciated. He sounds more like a father or a lover than a sibling or a friend. "Or did you talk about Ma—" A server comes with the rose wine Pollo ordered, and he falls quiet. Mel's eyes widen just to forget what she was thinking as soon as they find themselves alone again. "So how are the drugs?" he asks Mel, giving her attitude.

"Great," Mel says, unaffected by his negativity. "To drugs," and she raises her glass, taking a big gulp of wine unaccompanied by the others.

Pollo gives Artie a ferocious ogle, crossing his arms.

"What?" his sister finally asks.

"What do you mean what? Look at her!"

"So?"

"So where's my dose?" he asks enviously. "You always do that. You're such a cunt."

"CTFO, dude. CTFO."

"FOMO, though," Mel chuckles, sympathetic to Pollo.

But the twins don't say anything until well into the appetizers when Pollo tells Artie about how much one of their friends is charging some television producer for sex. Artie says she doesn't care about those people anymore, and Pollo caustically teases her about her new friends. Unaware he's referring to her, Mel tries to not look like a savage as she stuffs her mouth. A belly dancer enters their room, but Artie tells her no, giving her a fat tip.

"I don't know why you build anything," Pollo hiccups after finishing his third glass of wine, "if you're just gonna tear it all down."

"Celeste!" Artie nags when it tries to climb on the table.

Mel assumes Artie knows what he's talking about when his dear sister tells him to not call her stupid, that she's doing all she can. He doesn't understand what she has to go through every day. Tears get in the mix, but he knows her too well to buy it. She had thought that he meant there was nothing to fret about so she wasn't fretting. He badgers her because what she's doing is not what he meant. They make sideway glances towards Mel. Artie clearly has built a tolerance to these things, as Mel keeps sinking and sinking and sinking into nonsense.

13

The car veers left, white and red lights blurred in time-lapse. The Moroccan food goes up Mel's throat and she gags as she looks up from her unapologetic daze, dozing off again once Pollo regains control of the vehicle. Celeste jumps from the back to the front into Artie's arms. "Habits" comes on the radio, and Mel looks up again, the food going up again as well.

"Change it, please," she begs, the nausea worsening, and Artie tends to the music.

She stops when she encounters "You Keep Me Hangin' On" a few stations later. Mel wonders how they got to the freeway, where they're headed. It's cold with the windows down, but it feels good on Mel's cut, the bandage coming off with her bouncing head. Where's her cardigan? Oh, she wrapped it around her shoulders. Wait, this isn't her cardigan. After shuffling against the straining seatbelt, her socked foot comes into contact with a ball of cotton. She stretches hard and gets to it, pulling out a T-shirt with the tags on.

"Where are we going?" Mel asks, not wanting to talk over the song. But the twins stare straight on, revealing nothing. Artie lights a cigarette, automatically handing one to Mel. That's when Mel heeds her mouth tastes like an ashtray. "No, thank you." Artie puts it away. "You know, this song reminds me of my 'sort of' ex'—since he was my 'sort of' boyfriend' after all. Don't you hate that? Like, you can't reserve people like that without meaning to use them. Well, not use use, but you know, like, I could be being loved by someone else instead. And I wanna be loved. I don't care how cool it is to not believe in love anymore. Biliberal womanist faggots with their gender-lending transveganism postracially pansexing all over town...ruining romance for the rest of us! But anyhow, I tried to kill myself and Rodrigo, the guy, he fucking...man, he, like, I didn't tell him, but maybe he could tell. It's hard to know. He just sort of seemed like he didn't know what to do. It was kinda funny. Schadenfreudingly, of course." An itch behind the ear leads Mel to discover she's wearing a headband. She takes it off. Shiny red. "Here," she says, extending her arm, "this would look better on you." Artie takes it and puts it on, checking herself out on the sun visor mirror. The moment opportune, she retouches her red lipstick. "I thought you had such great style as a kid," Mel says with an air of nostalgia.

"You know," Artie starts, her voice shaky, "I don't remember that summer much."

From the back seat, Mel can hear Pollo's grip on the leather of the steering wheel cover stiffen. He drives a little too close to the wall on the carpool lane, the swish swish of Artie's constant toying of her pendant keeping time from side to side.

"Yeah, dude," Mel says as if the conversation mattered little, her tongue lazy. "It's insane how that happens."

"Yup," Artie agrees, nodding quickly, putting the tip of her cigarette out the window for the ash to get blown.

"I'm scared there's more to it. Like we watched a snuff film or something. I mean, supposedly my cousin let me watch *The Texas Chain Saw Massacre*."

"Yeah," says Artie after a pause. "That movie's effed up."

"And when you're a kid, I mean," Mel keeps going, "imagine that. See, I don't remember that part. My mom and dad have confirmed it, but I still...I still don't recall."

"Well, you were little."

"It's not that." Mel shakes her head.

"Then what is it?"

Through the soft focus, the flare, twinkling headlights of a calm night, as high as she is, Mel thinks she sees Pollo send Artie an I'm-gonna-kill-you look. Artie coughs and pretends she didn't ask anything, beginning to sing. Yet she doesn't use her talent, she just talks the words.

"But seriously, though—watch out!"

Without having ever looked away from the road, Pollo still checks all his mirrors, stepping on the breaks a tad as he makes sure that nothing's wrong.

"What?!" goes Artie. "What?!"

"You almost drove into a palm tree..." Mel lets out with a huff, noticing it was never there. She removes her glasses and attempts to clean them with the new cardigan, but it only rubs the dirt around. The car swerves again and the glasses fall on the floor.

"Jesus! What is up with people tonight?" Pollo goes angrily.

"It's L.A., darling."

"Not anymore."

Unable to see, Mel stares after the road signs, feeling around the floor with her feet for her glasses.

"Where are we going?" she asks one more time just so they can avoid responding. Even with all her current suspicion and paranoia, none of it equates to the warm feeling of being completely at ease. It's almost as if she's getting something important done, like she should be rewarded on the sole basis of having taken the benzos. Then the eyes begin to well up as customary when such happiness is achieved. "Actually, I'll, yeah, I'll have that cigarette..." Artie delivers with a jeer. "Muchas gracias."

The lighter shoots up a flame longer than Mel expected, for a second fearing she could have burnt her eyebrows. Managing to light the Superslim, she takes a long, dramatic drag. Her lungs fill with smoke and she grows even more lightheaded. The palm trees swoop past, one after the other after the other, the lane extending into the distance of that distant memory. "We won! We won!"

"We won, we won," Mel repeats to herself as if it were hilarious. "What was it?"

"Huh?"

"The thing. The thing we won."

"You mean the sandcastle competition?"

"Sandcastle—"

"Artie," Pollo announces flatly, demanding obedience.

"It was fixed! There! There you go! What's your goddamn obsession—" Artie hisses with no self-control, Celeste biting her thumb blithely.

"Artie!"

"Is that why I keep getting this mischievous feeling—"

"What? I'm just telling her! The poor bitch is going crazy. It was fixed. The competition was bullshit. My mom's friend was in charge of it and she let us win. You don't know moms. They have all these conspiracies and shit—"

"Are you serious—"

"Our castle was pretty dope though, wasn't it, Pollo?" Artie sputters apace. "Wasn't it?"

He changes lanes, concurring with an authorizing: "Mhm."

"How did you get used to your new names? Personally I like Tilly and Sam, Tilly and Sam, has a ring to it—argh!"

The repetition makes parts of her brain tingle.

"We're Tilly."

"And Sam."

Mel looks up again, the smothering coziness drooping her eyelids. Artie and Pollo never said anything. Maybe the dog barked.

"Where are we going?" But at this point it's irrelevant.

Letting her neck hang loose, Mel plummets into the vacuous hug waiting for her when she closes her eyes. She moans, rubbing the stolen cardigan on her cheek. And just like she forgot their escapade to American Apparel, the extra pills, so much peer pressure, the conversation they just had slowly starts to fog away. She swears she'll remember this one, but memory's clearly not her thing.

14

What seems like not even five minutes go by when the car comes to a complete stop, and, thrusting forward, Mel awaits the crash though it never comes. In fact, Pollo slowed the car down as properly as possible. Artie grabs him by the chin with her thin hands and forces him to face her.

"Cool," she tells him. "Keep it—"

"Cool, yeah, yeah," he says, freeing himself.

Barely able to keep one eye open, Mel sees the cop car behind them, the lights too bright to stare into. Perhaps she imagines it, but she can hear the footsteps on the rubble, the weight of weapons, the ever-present chewing gum. The Moroccan food starts going up again as Mel becomes nervous, finally reaching down to grab her glasses, uncertain where she lies in the whole situation. As far as she's concerned, she was drugged and dragged to wherever they're going, so, you know, kidnapped.

"License and registration please," orders the pig, and Pollo meets her with all the necessary paperwork.

"Is there anything wrong, officer?" asks the young man, puffing his chest.

"Sir, have you been drinking tonight?" she goes like clock-work, more intrigued by the dog.

"I had a glass of wine with dinner, yes," Pollo lies, a whole bottle consumed by him throughout the spread of an hour.

"You were wobbling a little back there."

"My GPS," he says frustrated, holding up his phone. "It got lost and it rerouted me like three times. I may have looked away from the road for a second or two, I apologize," he says suavely.

And it being the charm that it is, it works. The lady in blue gives him back his documents and waves him on goodbye, wishing him a wonderful night. Artie takes the stuff from him while he gets back on the 10 as if nothing had happened. Mel joins in the laughter, straightening her back, rewired by the trepidation. She takes both of them in as they keep on trucking, arguably happy for them. Artie's left hand thumbnail, expensively manicured, French tip, points to a younger Pollo, surfer-haired, bespectacled, a Samuel Timothy Bonham, or so the I.D. reads.

"Wait a minute...your name's still Samuel Timothy Bonham," Mel points out.

Pollo and Artie look at each other. Both pretty much just choose to overlook what they don't want to address. Some shady shit. The silence lingers on as the Audi S7 is taken to a hundred miles per hour. The speed, the glints, cops and robbers. Mel tries to leave one foot in reality, fixating on not throwing up, as her state of overload clouds her thinking. Everything shutters. 2001. Evil, pure evil. The same old thing. Degeneration after degeneration. Some sort of crying spell and thrusting, cameos, curved backs, bent legs, sweat, blood, all of it. "Tilly and Sam! Tilly and Sam!" The palm trees, so jubilant. "Night Mara! Night Mara!" No, no.

"Oh, no. No. No!"

Artie looks back and watches Mel's body writhe feverishly.

"Dude, I don't know what's wrong with her."

"What do you mean?" Pollo asks, taking a quick glance at the backseat. "Is she seizing?"

"No...just...she looks like she's in shock or something."

"Night Mara," Mel utters. "Night Mara."

She and Artie make eye contact. Mel opens her mouth and screams inwardly, tears forming in her eyes, her hands shaking in horror. Artie asks her: "What? What?!" But Mel just cries, seeing things that aren't there. Her heart races faster than it ever has, blinded by imagined eclipses, voices chanting inside her skull where they reverberate as her eyelashes flutter.

"What is wrong with you?!" Artie erupts, but she might already know exactly what. And that's good, for how could Mel put into words the darkness fading in, her brain bombarded with neurotransmitters and receptors that don't match. Here we lift the curtain, no matter how hard everyone tried in this great scheme.

In that fashion, the car ride stays free of conversation, the radio at maximum, Mel's quiet breakdown left alone in the back where she crinkles with her contorting joints.

The twins take the lunatic to their ward, a four bedroom home in Palm Springs. The driveway light turning on automatically, Pollo parks outside and they observe Mel, not even a toe left on this Earth. He grabs her giant purse and dips his arm in, searching through tissues and tampons and coins. "Goddammit. No cigarettes."

"I got you."

"You know I hate those." He comes across the Polaroid and pulls it out. Artie looks over, chuckling. "This is why?" he asks as if it were ridiculous.

"We've gotten better at not leaving a trail."

"I'm not so sure," he says upon finding the hit list. "Aren't you missing something?"

"What the fuck?! She went through my stuff?!" and she looks at Mel through the rear-view mirror.

"I told you to throw this thing away. It's not even accurate."

"'Cause I don't have your shit on it."

"Why don't you just move? You can still pay the rent."

"That's what I've been saying this whole time!"

"I thought you cared about your band—"

"Oh, come on. There is no band."

"Yeah, but before you still had that. Now there's no turning back. At all."

Flustered, they get out of the car, and Pollo goes ahead and grabs Mel by the armpits to haul her in. Artie goes for the feet, barely able to lift her.

"She's big," Artie grumbles as the five-foot-ten, hundred-forty-pound girl gets carried off clumsily.

Pollo lets her drop once inside, Mel still muttering, "Night Mara," over and over again under her breath. Artie tries smoking a cigarette, but Mel's talking keeps distracting her. The liquor cabinet is opened and Pollo pours two tequila shots, observing Mel on the floor callously.

"Oh my god, shut up!" Artie asks of Mel, but obviously Mel can't help her or herself.

Enraged, Artie looks around the living room for something sturdy. Here, a ceramic bud vase, probably worth a lot, made in Mexico, conk, right to the frontal lobe.

"Perfect."

"Is that the only way you know how to take care of things?" Pollo asks his sister arrogantly, watching her fidget with her jewelry.

"It worked then, it'll work now."

"We've caused her so much brain damage, the dumb broad," he laughs. "But some people just get in the way."

"Mhm."

They both nod, avoiding the body on their way for more Gran Patrón. Pollo switches on the picture lights, the wood paneling brightening, the carpet whitening. He unlaces his shoes and takes them off, throwing them at the backyard door. This is his residence: their mother's vacation home. She and Pollo haven't properly spoken in years—"Hello, son," "Goodbye, Mother"—but the fact that the electric bill still gets paid is their mutual agreement to remain family. Artie has a harder time with it, easily manipulated by Mother, battling her desire to sever all ties. Mostly she's just jealous Pollo can still play Sam, which isn't an option for her anymore. But as retired with their two thirds of Dad's money as they are, they opt to keep to themselves.

"I just watched the Nirvana Rock and Roll Hall of Fame thing."

"Did you like Lorde?" he asks, walking to the kitchen.

"Eh."

"I loved it," he has no problem admitting, returning with a baby blue dog leash. He kneels down by Mel and shoves her on her side, pulling her arms together behind her back to tie the wrists with the leash. After knotting it multiple times, her flesh turning dark red under rolls of pressure, he snatches her by the hair and leaves her face up in case she does end up throwing up. "I'm so full still."

"I ate so much tonight."

"Don't worry about it," and he gives her a loving peck on the lips.

He's the one that doesn't need to worry, his black leather pouch down the hall towards the end in the master bedroom in his dresser, third drawer, under the silk pajamas he only wears around Christmas. The wait isn't long, and after a shower of spewing bile down the drain, Artie passes out in her preferred guest room. The other one hasn't moved, her breathing steady but clamorous. If the belle's belfry doesn't fry fully, she might recollect some dream matter.

Leaving the rest for tomorrow, Pollo takes off the T-shirt they smuggled in Mel's giant purse out of the Studio City store, making his way to his quarters. The desert outside howls, the moon splendidly autumn bright as seen through the ample window atop his bed. He draws the curtains and unbuckles his belt, pulling it out of the loops. Takes a leak, takes off his contact lenses, takes his time making his way to the black leather pouch. The zipper comes undone, he opens it up, cooks it up, fixes himself up, and his mouth drops open once the release is initiated. Hustling the hours of the day to deserve, finally, a feeling. And there he stays.

15

"You let him get away with it!" He's never heard this screaming before, the jeans he left on becoming unbuttoned. "You bastard!" The sun's barely somewhere close to the horizon, keeping the room dark. The door is open. He thought he left it locked. What the fuck is happening? Pollo opens his eyes with great difficulty. "What?" he asks, whoever's on him giving him no answer. At first he worries it's Artie trying to get busy when he's obviously not in the mood, but it can't be her. The door was locked. Artie can't open doors that are locked. "How did you get in?"

"Butter knife," replies the other person.

"But how—how—"

"Double jointed," the villain lays out.

"No—what—" he goes, sitting up too slowly for his deranged opponent who struggles to wiggle the clothes out of him. "What are you doing?"

"Someone's gotta pay, Sam."

"What?"

"He died years ago in a drunken car crash. You're just as guilty. Someone's gotta pay."

She manages to get the pants off him, proceeding to rip apart his underwear from the waistband, leaving him in his black Polo socks. He starts to freak out, picking the needle out of his arm, raising it above his head at the assailant.

"Mel?" But he can't strike fast enough, and Mel takes the syringe, throwing it far into the bathroom, hitting the wall and disappearing somewhere behind the toilet. "What are you doing—"

"He raped her, Sam!"

"No, no, that's not what—" he says, fighting the drowsiness for his life. "He—he—she should've known it would hurt—"

"And you mother fuckers closed the door and—"

"No, no, you don't get it—"

The voice most of us hear as we're about to make decisions, whether big or small, that thing called judgment, that voice is gone. All Mel sees now is the past, guided hysterically by the instinct to atone. They were responsible for what went down that summer, Tilly and Sam cantillating, "Night Mara!" to the beat of a beating.

"Mel!" he begins to beg. "No! Please, no!"

"Rapist," she croons. "Rapist!"

"But I didn't—we were—we were kids, dammit! Aaah!"

She holds on to the ceramic bud vase trying to get at him, to get him, and him in his haze, crying distantly for help, dodges what he can see coming from the distance of a breath. So far the only ears that perk are those of a pack of coyotes strutting nearby on their way to their den after a successful hunt. They don't concern themselves with civilization. Obdurate life, creating for the sake of creating, atrocious behavior in the human realm where out of what we can afford to confuse for those same needs, worse things happen.

And just when the struggle is about to take off, the lights turn on. Pollo and Mel make eye contact briefly, he trying to recover from his nakedness, she measuring how much more ravaging she can get.

"Get the fuck away from him!"

Standing with her legs spread without crossing the threshold, Chihuahua at her feet, Artie seems to have awakened, a silver snub-nosed revolver in her hand. She points it at Mel as steadily as she can, never having fired a gun before. But that's just one of Artie's secrets, and when Mel becomes aware of the new plight, she's as terrified as she should be. Pollo scurries bunglingly off the bed, crashing knees first on the rug. He moves at his own pace in rags, making it to the bathroom where he can lock himself in, his exhausting yowling still audible.

Wrapping her head around the fact that she's not the only mad one, Mel takes a step forward. Celeste snarls through Artie's legs.

"So a—a—are you gonna shoot me, or wha—at?" Mel breaks the silence with a quake, moving towards her a bit more. "'Cause you're blo—blocking the exit."

Attempting to cock the gun, Artie messes with it and misfires, shooting the settee to Mel's left. The bang deafens all of them, scaring the shit out of Celeste who darts across the room right into Mel's reach. Nimble even though she's not herself, Mel trails after it and snatches it by the belly.

Rational now that there's a hostage, Artie walks backward down the hall and into the living room where Mel follows her, neither of them saying anything, Artie's finger on the trigger, Mel's hands around the pup's neck. Here Artie lowers the weapon, climbing on the couch and reaching into the already open safe to start taking out stacks of money, throwing them at Mel whose reflexes quit working and doesn't catch them, not getting what's going on. Artie keeps hitting her in the face with cash until it seems like enough to secure herself and her family unharmed. She even finds Pollo's car keys on the bar and these, too, fly at Mel, getting her on the stomach.

"Take it!" Artie yells, tripping over the painting she removed from the wall. "Take it! Go!"

Mel's grip fastens. It takes her a while, though eventually she bends over deliberately to pick up the keys. Artie starts feeling relieved, the snubbie in her non-dominant hand, the right one ready to welcome her precious baby back. However, after organizing her thoughts, a good moiety of her body already outside, Mel holds Celeste up before her with both hands like a ritual and in a long, painful moment, crack, the hairy body snaps, landing by Mel's feet where she goes one step further and kicks it at Artie. She sticks around to watch the mother's world end, and then she's out the door hurrying into the S7, dodging a few bullets.

The car reverses as it ticks five in the morning, her foot solidly on the gas beginning to feel odd. Rolling through a stop sign, Mel feels around her thigh until she finds the itch. It bleeds through the fabric, the scrape giving her jeans a modern edge. In that fickle frenzy, the epinephrine and the norepinephrine and the serotonin and the dopamine, she finds the main road as someone must inevitably be calling the cops on the disarrayed dwelling.

Commoving behind the wheel on lonesome Palm Canyon Drive, she halts alongside a fire hydrant to let some clarity dawn on her. "Siri?" she calls out, seeking to find her cell phone. At last she digs into the mess of the backseat and retrieves it from the giant purse she conveniently left there along with her shoes. "Nearest hospital."

Going twenty miles an hour, the navigational system directs her into the parking lot where she double parks and hurries along the path to the emergency room, cold in her new cardigan, her Converse halfway in. With no one else there, Mel goes up to the window. A few minutes go by as she remains unattended.

"And the reason for your visit?" asks the bubbly receptionist after she's finished filling out the forms, most of the questions remaining unanswered.

"I—I don't really know," she explains to the nurse before this one can check out her forehead as she gets IVed. "I can—I can tell I'm, uh, hallucinating? 'Cause it can't be...my—my—my heart's pounding out of my chest, I mean—I can't see, I can't breathe, I can't think. I can't think!" she elaborates to the doctor so he may approve a second dose of Ativan without any more delay.

Someone lays a blanket atop her as the medicine spreads. The goose bumps flatten down, the melancholy relieves, and coming off one thing, going up another, soon the monomania subsides, and she gives out a gargling snuffle, capsizing further into the root of her problem.

16

The ride from Riverside to Santa Monica is a long one when you don't even remember getting ready before being strapped to the car, carsickness keeping you awake. Mel sits restlessly listening to her CD player, a burnt copy of *The Marshall Mathers LP* spinning without scratches. Palm trees lead the way until all Mel can see out the window above her are the swaying green leaves taller than any mansion. Purely mesmerizing.

The previous year, when it was too soon to be thrown into a life with her dad's new girlfriend—Mel thought it had something to do with the fact that she's black—Mel's mom drove her to Thousand Oaks to stay at her grandparents' house for the summer. There she met her future stepmom, Carine, and stepsister, Mara. At the time, Mara was still just a kid, and she played with Mel no problem—although she was over the whole Barbie thing, she had a PlayStation so they were okay.

But when Mel gets dropped off on Adelaide Drive a year later—her mother never steps into the front yard—and is greeted by her dad, Carine, and her grandparents, Mel asks about Mara, but this one doesn't take the time to come say hello.

"She's upstairs," Carine says as if she'd tried before and had to learn there's no winning with her daughter.

Mel finds twelve too soon to start acting like a teenager, yet that's all Mara does. She wears a disgustingly old blue flannel shirt—probably her dad's—where dirt gathers at the cuffs, and is never seen without headphones. Even when they go to the beach later, there with her curves developing underneath, she shies away in a one-piece and the flannel shirt and headphones. What could she be listening to? Carine says it's a bunch of noise. Mara sees what Mel listens to and says: "That song, 'The Real Slim Shady,' is funny to sing along to 'cause then you are imitating and the joke's on you." Mel stops singing altogether.

At the beach, Mel carries buckets of water back to her spot so she can work on a sandcastle. The bits of skin where she missed to put on sunscreen—she's old enough to do it herself now—start getting red as Carine and Herman run into some friends, and they get talking. Mel watches deep in thought, her eyes behind sunflower-shaped sunglasses. Herman points at Mel while he says something to the man, and the older gentleman calls out somewhere close by. Soon enough, two kids appear at their parents' side.

"She's a bit of a loner," Herman says. "If I don't make friends for her, she'll be playing alone all summer."

Mel hears this, so she gets ready for what's next. He's always interfered with her wishes, like that of keeping to herself. In her experience, kids are cruel. Not any worse than adults, just people. People in general are bad.

The boy and girl do as instructed and approach Mel.

"Hi," says the girl straightforwardly. "We're Tilly."

"And Sam," adds the boy.

"What's up?" she says comically.

"Just working on this," Mel answers, looking at her droopy sandcastle.

Tilly twists the ruby pendant hanging from a white gold chain around her neck from side to side. She's wearing big heart-shaped sunglasses and a white bikini revealing her baby fat tummy, the bellybutton sunken in. Her light brown hair's in a ponytail, a red ribbon tied around it falling behind her. Even the nails on her fingers and toes are red. Sharp.

"I like your sunglasses," she says to Mel.

"Thanks. I like yours."

"They're Lolita sunglasses. You know what that is?" Mel shakes her head politely. "It's from a movie."

"A book," Sam corrects her.

"Not the sunglasses," Tilly reminds him.

He exhales miffed, his muscles flexing when he switches his posture. He's got long hair for a boy, just like his sister's, but otherwise they look nothing alike. Taller and fitter, Sam stands behind Tilly as if protecting her from harm.

"Our parents told us to come play with you."

"You don't have to if you don't wanna."

"Nah, we were bored anyway," Tilly says, sitting under the striped umbrella Herman planted claiming the land. A little bit more skeptical, Sam does the same. "There's gonna be a sandcastle building competition in a couple of days. Ages six to twelve. How old are you?"

"I'll be eight on Sunday."

"Perfect. We're ten. I'll tell our mom to sign us up."

"Are you good at it?"

"Well, you're pretty decent. But don't worry, our mom is friends with the lady organizing it. We just needed a third person. Three to six people per group."

"Sounds fun."

Sam opens his mouth to speak but thinks better of it. The action makes Tilly antsy. She grabs one of the molds and fills it with wet sand.

"Are you Carine's stepdaughter?" Tilly asks, faking to be busy.

"My dad and her aren't married."

"But, you know, casually."

"I guess."

"Are you staying at her house?"

"Yeah. Why?"

"Then we know where you're at," says Tilly with a naughty grin. "We're just down the street."

Tilly's friendliness starts to bother Mel who'd rather be alone again. She simply doesn't like being asked all these questions. What does she need to know for anyway? They just met.

A few yards away, Mel sees Carine nag at Mara while the gal complains. Carine says something about the flannel shirt, then attempts to take it off her daughter without getting too physical, but Mara reverts. She walks away from her mother and sits flatly on her ass, readjusting her headphones to listen to whatever and take in the ocean. The twins look in her direction.

"So you know Mara." Tilly says to Mel.

"Yup."

"She's kinda weird, huh?"

"Not really," Mel says a bit defensively. "She's all right."

"What do you think she's listening to?"

"I don't know."

"What do you listen to?"

"Hip-hop mostly."

Sam throws Mel a look of disbelief, but he quickly turns away, crossing his arms as if cold. Mel observes it's not as hot as everyone makes it seem. Two tall young women with bronze skin and wet hair in tiny bathing suits walk by. The twins stare after them drunk with puberty. Meanwhile Mel removes one of the molds, a perfect tower now standing. She takes the broken pieces of beer bottle she found earlier and places them along the walls. There. Stained glass windows.

A beeping suddenly erupts from one of the picnic bags. After a few seconds, Herman rapidly makes his way to the sound and answers his mobile phone. "Yeah, hello?" He stays there nodding with, "Uh-huhs," until finally he hits end and bites his finger.

Carine looks at him expecting something. "My brother's at your house."

"What?" Carine responds, walking towards him, readjusting her bracelets.

"Wesley," Herman says concerned, "just got to your house. My mother called."

"So are they coming?" Carine asks innocently.

"No." Herman smoothes down his eyebrows from the center and down the sides of his face with one nervous movement, ending up at his teeth again. "I think we have to go."

Upon hearing these words, Mel makes an assessment of how long it will take her to pack all her goods and sprint. Forty seconds at most. As Herman and Carine discuss this, Mel gives Tilly and Sam the smile of a goodbye.

"Mara!" Carine finally calls out to her daughter a ways away.

Mel gets up and slaps the sand off her hands, ignoring Tilly and Sam while she gathers the shovels and buckets and molds.

"You're leaving?" Tilly asks a bunch of times.

"Yeah, yeah," Mel murmurs absent-mindedly.

Herman folds the towels as Mel stands all ready to go. He closes his eyes, tired of these things. His kid is not gonna be some antisocial little shit like his brother's. Fucking hell, and now they're in that house waiting. Talk about a bad omen.

The car gets full of sand and Mel has to sit on a towel but the seat still gets wet. "I went in like half an hour ago!" she holds her own when Herman scolds her. "I didn't think I was that wet!"

Angrier now, Herman carries the bags and umbrella back into the garage, his crowded front teeth showing. He can hear Carine entering the kitchen.

"Carine!" goes that voice feigning pizzazz as if he knew the woman well. "Beautiful as always."

"Wesley," Carine says like oh please.

"I was talking to Ma and she says: we're all staying at Carine's near the beach for a couple of weeks. Family gathering, she says. So how could I miss it?"

Carrying her toys in a large plastic bag, Mel enters the garage, interrupting Herman. He gives the child a scowl, then goes into the house.

"How did you know where we were?" is the first thing he says.

Mel follows suit. There they are: Wesley and Junior AKA Wes. Robustly built, buzz-haired, frowning, father and son in the kitchen wearing jeans and plain black T-shirts, the older one's face covered in wrinkles, the younger one's in pimples.

"Ma gave me the address," Wesley says to his brother, feeling accused of wrongdoing.

"Then how come she called me saying you were here out of nowhere-like?" Herman asks, staring at their mother.

Lisa shrugs her shoulders, stating: "I thought it was a family gathering."

"So you drove all the way from..." Carine gets lost.

"Oxnard," Wesley finishes for her.

"Oxnard, Oxnard."

"You got the beach over there, why you gotta come over here?" Herman questions him from the other side of the room. Carine hands Wesley a beer and he thanks her dutifully, staring at her ass when she turns around. He looks at his brother in an acknowledging way, repulsing Herman. "But I'm afraid there's no room. The guest room's taken."

"I'm sure we can figure something out," Carine says sweetly, perhaps overly so.

"Yeah, what she said," says Wesley vulgarly, taking a seat next to Lisa. He puts his hand on her knee. She shakes it away. "Can't cancel the wedding just 'cause there's a little bit of rain, can ya?"

"Is that a real saying?" Mel asks.

Herman closes his eyes and slightly moves his head from side to side. Mel comprehends. She avoids Uncle Wesley's eyes and accidentally bumps into Wes'. He's a character, Mel would like to think. She's never hung out with him much before, the age difference too great. But Wesley and Wes are hardly ever present when she visits her dad's family anyway. It must have something to do with Wesley's wife having left when Wes was a little boy. For some reason, that topic is never brought up, so it must be that. But as much as Mel wonders what it's like to go through that, to be unwanted by a parent, it's impossible for her to feel how Wes feels, try to understand him, try to help him out. He just stands there by the dishwasher, breathing through his mouth, brown eyes black.

A man's hand on her shoulder starts leading Mel out of the kitchen. She looks up at Herman as they enter the dining room.

"Go take a shower and get all the sand out. Leave your swimsuit in the shower after washing it. And your flip flops. Get in the shower with them on, let them get washed, and then leave them there. Don't walk out in your wet flip flops—"

"Yeah, okay, okay," Mel says irritated.

She goes upstairs through the living room, leaving a trail of beach stuff on the maroon carpeted steps. Finding Mara's door closed—a blue sign reading "Night Mara" hanging from a nail—she knocks a few times. Since there's no answer, she goes ahead and enters, going straight for the see-through telephone.

"Mom?"

Mother offers advice on homesickness, dad-tolerating, and friend-making.

"Oh yeah? And what are their names?

"Tilly and Sam."

"What?"

"Tilly and Sam!"

The door opens and Mara mopes in. Mel quickly hangs up and pretends she wasn't doing anything. Mara plays along. She kicks off her sandals and throws herself on the bed—no regard for how filthy she is—grabbing a pack of Juicy Fruit from the night table drawer.

"Can I have one?"

Mara throws a piece at Mel without saying a word, reaching under the bed to pull out a Rolling Stone with The Rock on the cover. She blows a bubble and puts on her headphones, then withdraws from the world for a while. Mel leaves her alone by taking that shower.

Grandma Lisa roasts a chicken, slices the gurkensalat real thin, and mashes a bunch of potatoes with the help of Carine who also works on a buttered rum pound cake. The men sit at the dinner table, Grandpa Johnny sipping on vino, Wesley on his sixth beer, Herman chewing on his finger. The kids are rounded up in the kitchen and made to sit there. Wes waits for the women to leave to grab himself a porter. He takes his first gulp and belches. Mara can't help but giggle. He does it again. She giggles once more.

After dinner, Mara takes them upstairs to the playroom and invites Wes to play *Final Fantasy*. Meanwhile Mel attempts to teach herself how to play pool, climbing the table to reach for the cue ball.

"Why do you have a—a—a poster of *Cha—Charlie's Angels*? That movie sucks," goes Wes uncalled for with his dumb stutter.

"'Cause they're super hot," Mara discloses matter-of-factly.

"Ew, are you ga—gay?"

"I don't have to be a lesbian to find women attractive."

"Bu—but do you just think they're ho—ho—hot or do you wanna bang them?"

"A little bit of both," Mara laughs. "Would you bang them?"

"Yeah. But I'm a gu—guy."

"Really?" Mara teases. Wes doesn't laugh. "Have you ever?"

"What?"

"Done it," she spits out harshly.

"Ye—yeah, well, almost."

"Who with?"

"This girl."

"What's her name?" Mara follows with briskly.

"Uh—A—Angela."

"Is she your girlfriend?"

"Yeah," Wes says from the side of his mouth, his nose twisted.

"Oh yeah?" Mara asks unashamed of her dubiety.

"Ye—yeah."

"Is she hot?"

"Super hot."

"So you haven't given it to her yet?" There's a pause. Mara snaps her gum twice and exhales, excited to hear his response. But Wes's eyes go from the floor to the wall to the ceiling, his answer an obvious no. "How far have you gone?"

"Far enough," he says flushing.

"Boobs?"

"Yeah, I've—ve touched them."

In between breaths, Mara softly murmurs: "You're full of crap," but he doesn't hear her.

Yet even with these notions that Wes isn't reliable a source, Mara warms up to his teenage angst and smiles wide, a piece of gum sticking out of one side of her mouth. Mel accidentally gets the eightball in the hole but it's the first time she gets one in so it's all right with her.

About two hours of coquetting go by before the adults show up upstairs with orders for the young ones. Brush your teeth, put on your pajamas, read a book, etcetera. Carine calls the Bonhams to see if they have an inflatable mattress she can borrow, and fifteen minutes later she and Herman are back with an unopened box. Wesley blows it up in the playroom while Wes takes the large leather couch. Herman passes the twins' regards onto Mel, then tucks her in even though she's not at all tired.

When he and Carine leave the room, Mara takes out a flashlight and resumes reading her Rolling Stone, another piece of gum in her mouth. There in the light of the blued peach-colored walls, Mara thinks about her day and certain thoughts make her down parts tingle. She's never understood where these tickles come from, but they go away if you press really hard against the pubic arch for a few seconds. It feels pretty good actually, like a stretch. She'd keep going, but that's something else.

On a mattress on the floor, Mel believes there's a change in rhythm to Mara's sleeping movements. Her breathing slows down, becoming deeper and louder through her clogged nose. The sound prevents Mel from falling asleep, but eventually her need for slumber overcomes all her senses.

17

It's no one's job to wake up Mel, so she sleeps until about twelve thirty when Mara comes in the room to put on shoes.

"We're going to the pier," she tells the still brain dead one rubbing her eyes open. "Get ready."

Mel sets them all back when she needs to get dressed, wash her face, brush her hair, but come on, come on already, and Herman yanks her by the strap of her teddy bear backpack. Carine calls Mara into the kitchen and Grandma and Grandpa shuffle into their car while Wes waits for Wesley who's in the bathroom. Mel sits in the back of her dad's car and watches Wes repeatedly look at his watch. When Mara comes out carrying a bag of food, he tries to take it from her, but she denies his help, it not being that big or heavy in the first place. He sticks around behind her until she gets in the car and closes the door. That's when Wes gets the hint that he should board too, his dad already in Grandpa's Buick. They all wait composed for about five minutes when Herman finds it odd that Carine is still inside. Maybe she needs help, he thinks, so he gets out and makes his way to her.

The girls stay in the car. Mel can make out the fast beat coming out of Mara's headphones melodized with savage, salvaging screaming. Sometimes she doesn't change the CD for hours, just keeps listening on repeat. The person responsible has gotta be Mara's fantastic, short-haired, tattooed, older half-sister who supported the Riot Grrrl movement in college. Carine doesn't appreciate any of it, but neither has she given it a chance. As for Mara, well, the message flies way over her tween head. Let's put it this way, she enjoys those comedy movies that make fun of fat people and teases her friends about them liking guys more popular than them since they don't stand a chance, and at the end of the day, with her blue flannel shirt trailing after her, the long mane of sun-bleached brown hair the same tone of her stretching skin, she's a shallow, sarcastic, insecure girl who bites her fingernails and promises she washes her hair when sometimes she simply wets it and reads some articles on the toilet with the shower running.

The minutes grow wearisome like they do when you're a kid and you're strapped to the seat and the scrapes on your knees itch and your scrunchy isn't tight enough.

"What are you doing?" Mara asks when Mel opens the door.

"Just checking."

Not caring, Mara lets Mel bravely walk back inside and into the kitchen. There she sees Herman holding on to Carine with her weight barely on a stool, something rigidly in her hand. They seem expectant.

"Can't keep her in the dark like this anymore. What if I'm not here one day?" Herman says almost inaudibly.

"What's wrong?" Mel asks innocently, not opening the door all the way.

Carine makes a motion to get her out of there, and Herman turns to his daughter with a pleading look that says I'll tell you later. So Mel waits outside the kitchen one minute, two minutes, three minutes, then peaks her head a little. Carine is whispering to Herman, looking rather unwell. She hears a sound and spots Mel again. This time she reacts sharply.

"Tell her to wait outside!" she commands. It upsets Herman, siding with his kid at the moment. "Just go!" she yells at Mel when neither of the Nicchis do as they're told.

On her way out to the driveway, Mel runs into an alarmed Mara, one headphone off.

"What's going on?" she asks in a manner that indicates she's used to secrecy.

"I think your mom's sick."

Mara attempts to go through Mel to the kitchen, but the smaller one extends her arm from one side of the door frame to the other.

"What the hell?"

"No one can go in."

"What do you mean?"

"Your mom said so—"

But Mara pays no mind and pushes her way through Mel— which Mel finds pretty mean for Mara's good nature towards her—and immediately starts demanding answers.

"Get out of here!" Carine can be heard yelling.

"But what is going on?!" goes Mara.

"Don't you take that tone with me!"

"What should I tell the others?" asks Herman, the only tranquil voice in the vicinity.

"I don't know, I don't know," answers his loved one.

"We're staying," he says once he gets to Grandpa's car. "Carine's not feeling too well and she'd rather postpone."

Unseen, Mel goes around the house to peek into the kitchen. Carine is taking deep breaths with her head low. Grandma Lisa comes in, and Carine clutches a small colorful makeup pouch, hiding it behind her back. Lisa puts some bags back and attempts talking to Carine, but Carine appears to be tired. When the elder lady exits, Carine puts the pouch under her arm and leaves slowly, her high-maintenance afro bouncing after her.

Without saying anything about whatever it was that happened, Grandma prepares lunch and Grandpa and Wesley watch TV while Mara takes Wes upstairs. Mel tries to keep up with the youngsters, but Herman takes her aside.

"Are you let down that we're not going to the pier?" Mel shrugs. "How about those kids yesterday? Did you like them? They seemed nice."

"They asked me to join their sandcastle building team."

"That's great! We should go to the beach and practice," he exclaims, more enthused than any other father would have been. He puts his hand up for a high five but Mel takes too long. By the time she raises her hand, Herman's already played it off. "See? It's good to be friendly."

"I am friendly."

"Not always."

"Uh—"

"You see your cousin Wes?"

"Yeah."

"You don't wanna be like that."

"Okay," she says, already over the conversation.

"Do you understand what I'm trying to tell you?" he says, kneeling to get on her level. "You wanna be nice. You want people to like you."

"He gets along with Mara."

"Well, that's because Mara's a little..." he leaves it at that. Grandpa Johnny calls him and he stands up. "All right, Mel?"

Mel nods, ignorant of the lesson she was supposed to learn.

The railing around the stairs is endless under Mel's dirty palms. Once in the playroom, she again feels the solitude of being too budding when she finds Mara and Wes playing pool. "Can I play?" Mel asks, but they laugh at her, thinking she was kidding.

Idly Mel ends up in Mara's bedroom going through her CD collection. She has a lot, but Mel doesn't recognize any of the bands except for what airs on MTV. There is one case open atop the dresser with the CD missing: *Sleater-Kinney*. A few books are stacked up next to the CDs where Mara also keeps her magazines. In front of her white desk, there is a corkboard covered in dozens of cut-out rock stars, photo booth pictures, and movie theater tickets, each with the names of those friends or relatives Mara went with scribbled on with a happy face or a heart. Mel opens the closet and doesn't find much besides jeans and T-shirts. Nothing she can prance around in.

The boredom is torture for Mel. No one gives her the time of day, there's no food she can snack on after lunch, and her father keeps telling her things like, "Act nice," and, "Say please." Finally, once she's feeling up to it, Carine gives Herman the Bonhams' number so he can invite the twins over for a play date. They enter confidently after having been there once before and go straight for the stairs to where the kids should be located. Sam knocks on the door, Tilly jumps in.

"Hello, gang!"

Their visit unannounced, Mel gets to her feet in the midst of gratefulness, devastation, and indifference. Cartoons play while Wes gets the striped six in the hole.

"What are you? We're English and French and Finnish," Tilly says, trying to make conversation.

"My dad's family's Italian and German, and my mom's from South America. Jewish."

"That's cool. What about you, Mara? Where are your people from?"

Mara is not amused. All the way across the pool table, she swallows a large gulp of I-can't-believe-this.

"My people?"

"Yeah."

"Do you even realize how racist that is?" Mara says, leaving the cue stick against the wall and turning after her long curly hair out of the door.

"What?" Tilly asks Mel. Mel inhales through her mouth. "I thought she was half white."

"She is," Mel confirms. "But what—"

"People are so touchy," Tilly concludes, grabbing Mara's cue stick with one hand, restlessly fingering the ruby pendant with the other from side to side. "You're winning, right?" she asks Wes. "I'm not very good myself," and she gets ready to miss. "I hope you're ready for the competition," Tilly says to Mel as Wes almost makes another.

The game continues for a few more rounds until Tilly gets an itch to glance sideways and she sees her brother standing there without much to do, pool not being one of his favorites apparently. Mel tries to get his attention and maybe play a game or two on the PlayStation, but he's Tilly's loyal bitch. Wes makes another ball, and Tilly takes that one deep breath that ends the game.

"What do you guys wanna play?" she asks, leaving the cue stick on the table, not a glance at her adversary. Sam sighs humidly, the rest of them capitulating to the mansion-cooled heat of being a useless summer child. "What about spin the bottle?" she offers mischievously.

"That's gross," goes Wes. "She's my—my cousin and you're si—siblings."

"But what about Mara?"

Tilly looks in a circle before going into the hallway. Sam instinctively follows, and Mel follows him, therefore Wes follows her. They come to the backyard where Tilly has found a softball bat. She bangs it on the floor a few times before Mara comes running from the kitchen to stop her.

"What in the world are you doing?!"

Carine comes out and checks. No one's hurt. Back in.

"Mara, would you kiss Wes?" Tilly asks, throwing the bat into a bush.

"What?"

"Would you?"

It's an awkward moment. Mara gets stuck without air for a few seconds while Wes unwillingly gawks at her from bottom to top. Firm legs, wide hips, a handful of breast. Her expression first goes from an ew to an oh, crossing eyes with him all lost in his own pangs of despised love. But would she? Unlike the Bonham twins who just have to grow out of stupidity, get a college degree and a tailored suit, Wes's ovate features and yolky movements are more of a permanent situation. The short eighteen-year-old could easily go through life receiving no love if it were up to his charisma. And so that's when Tilly and Sam come in.

"Would you? Would you?"

"They're wimps, Til. Leave them be."

"I don't get why. We kiss all the time."

"What?"

Mara looks at Wes, but his blank reaction is not what she's looking for. She switches to Mel, but Mel is going through a lot more stress in the current situation, the whole kissing thing kind of a big deal to her.

"Look," Tilly says nonchalantly, her grimy sandaled feet approaching the white sneakers of her brother. Standing still, Sam welcomes her into his space and, lowering his head, they peck on the lips. "See?"

But what the twins see is Mara's mouth wide open, her eyelid shaking in shock. "That is so wrong," she mouths, unable to stand up to the crazies.

"Come on, Mara," Sam pressures her, his desire to corrupt more valuable than preserving his detached aura. "Just do it."

"Haven't you ever kissed anyone before?"

"What do you care?" Mara responds, but as hostile as she gets with the tone of her voice, she stays.

"She hasn't," Sam tells Tilly.

Who are you and who the hell do you think you are talking about me in front of my face, Mara stops herself from saying, but

Wes is still pulsating next to her. She had wanted to kiss a boy before, many times, many boys, but never like this. She wanted moonlight and rain, a soft cheek's caress, feet heeled, hair pinned, and the mollifying of a swain's eyes upon processing what just happened. Oh the luck of being kissed by a pretty girl in the lonely world of misunderstood men, their arms of steel too clumsy to mend the delicate fractures of their hearts.

And then there's Wes.

If she knew who Wes is, maybe her opinion would sway. But not even Wes knows who he is, or what he feels, or how he urges in his dreams but then the alarm goes off and it's all the same. Walking on sand, beach sunsets stir the dogs rowdy at night, the dead dogs of morning. Jack on the side, fetished, buying cigarettes for Dad. Neither expected anything out of the boy's life, and the elder watched him fail and fail until it was cheaper to keep him around lazy, reminding him at every opportunity what a loser he is. Junior stared at him with the same amount of rage and ordered him to shut up. A beer bottle flew past his head, hitting the wall. But it doesn't always hit the wall. Determined, the youngin crept into the master bedroom around three in the morning and watched his father sleep for as long as he could. When his thoughts took him to the place he thought he wasn't capable of going, he forgot to be quiet and ran back to his room. The drunkard never found out.

And then there's Mara.

"Come on," Sam says once more. "Just do it."

A homely smirk crosses the two potential lovers' faces and to the kids' imposition they bend. Wes takes his hands out of his pockets, Mara wets her lips, and in less than a second their mouths share an electric shock, strange for summer.

The children awe beyond themselves. The twins almost have to wipe off the drool off their chins if they didn't actually do so discretely. Mel finds it odd how easy the undertaking ended up being. It could be she sensed the disappointment, how Mara went back to standing far away from him and Wes simply took it.

"Ha!" Tilly teases them, her and her brother's pride at the point where they become the leaders of this group, however old they are.

"I've done w—worse things," Wes confesses. "I've killed, you know?"

The other four fall silent.

"Like hunting?" Sam asks.

"You co—could call it that," Wes threatens.

Mara pulls on the sleeve of her flannel shirt. So she's being compared to killing for sport, so what?

Heavily making his way out, establishing his upcoming presence so as to not take the children by surprise—he understands kids like maintaining secrecy—Herman takes his time before knocking on the open glass door, putting an end to their shenanigans.

"Let's go to the beach," he says, and everyone's on board.

His belly, decorated in a small T-shirt so he can avoid putting on sunscreen, protrudes as Herman picks a spot where the sand is at a good consistency for building. They all spread out and he starts giving orders, you there fetch water, you over here dig a hole, and the tanned little bodies move about creating a magnificent palace. But as the courts get bigger and more rooms are added—another wing for the princess for she's a lover of literature and has a personal library of fifty thousand volumes— Mara leaves, followed by Wes. Mel watches them talk about something they seem to disagree on as Tilly and Sam get bored of Herman's perfectionism. Only Mel remains when Carine stops by and snaps a picture of the colossus. The tide gets closer and father and daughter Nicchi watch their creation get destroyed with that certain pleasure the two of them share.

Tilly and Sam stick around for dinner—even after Mel bought them ice cream and candy from the neighborhood ice cream and candy truck with money she found in the junk drawer in the kitchen—but Grandma Lisa, who is for some reason put in charge of the children, isn't keen on them. They keep getting off their seats and telling inappropriate stories about this time they saw a dead hobo in New York and about their mother's butt implants. "Be quiet, for God's sake!" pleads Grandma, emphasizing the capital G most sacredly. The devils don't listen.

"Are you rich too?" Tilly questions Mel out of the blue, food in her mouth, her hand going for her glass of soda.

"What do you mean?" Mel asks, beginning to feel uncomfortable.

"Does your dad have dough like Carine's ex husband?" Tilly clarifies.

"Oh, I don't think so."

"How come you don't know? Doesn't he talk about his job?"

"You're asking how much he gets paid, not what he does," Mel responds.

"Does your mom work?"

Feeling threatened, Mel holds her tongue when suddenly Carine enters, grabs something from the fridge, and goes back to the adults without ever acknowledging them. Tilly asks again, and Mel ignores her. When Tilly's about to repeat herself one more time, Sam throws her a look and she retreats. When the silence gets awkward, Tilly tells Mel about their forthcoming summer camp. She loses Mel when she starts describing how much the camp costs plus everything they had to buy, her fingers crassly shoving food in her mouth every other sentence.

Mr. and Mrs. Bonham come by shortly afterward and stay for a glass of wine. "Ugh," goes Mel as the twins have to stay longer, tired of them already. They keep talking about stuff, about things, criticizing anything they don't understand, laughing at their inside jokes like they're so cute. When it's time to leave, they don't say thank you, talking smack on the play date in Mel's hearing range to their incurious mother, their haughty father, all the way up the street to their lofty house where they, indolently as usual, wish to be back at Carine's.

"I don't really like them," Mel says to Herman, following him to the kitchen.

"Who?"

"Tilly and Sam."

"What are they called again?"

"Tilly and Sam, Tilly and Sam," Mel answers desperately. "You're so bad with names."

"And faces." He throws out the last of the wine and places the bottle in the trash. "Take this out, will you?" Mel nods, knotting the bag twice. Then she looks up. "It's right by the garage door," he instructs, and she starts walking towards the backyard. "Give them a chance, Mel. It takes time to make friends with someone."

"I guess," she gives up, bowing slightly before hurrying on out to the bins.

On her way back in, the moon shines in an angle that shows Mel what she just ignored on her walk this way: a black widow on her web amidst the fence and a tree. The thought of killing it occurs to her, but she's no match for it. As she's about to crouch and go under it, she thinks better of it, going around to the front door. She rings the bell, convincing herself that she let the spider live out of respect.

Yawning, Mel gets in her sleeping bag around her official bedtime, which is rare. She leaves the lamp on for Mara's return. Today was weird. Oh well. All shall be amended soon.

18

"Happy birthday to you! Happy birthday to you! Happy birthday, dear Melainaaa! Happy birthday to you!"

Mel forces her eyes open, attempting to focus them on her beaming father. He kneels down and sets a tray at the foot of her mattress. Mara's bed is unmade, the window open, a car rolling by. Herman hugs her limply and brings out one of the plates with two bagels on it .

"Get it? It's an eight," he says to her awfully cheerfully, tempering with her morning grumpiness.

"What time is it?"

"Eight."

"What?!"

"Come on, it's funny!" She shakes her head without sharing the excitement as he takes his bagel, biting into it. "Besides, you got that competition at ten. You don't wanna miss that."

"That's today?"

"Yup."

"I don't really wanna do it."

"Mel, you never stick to anything. The Bonhams are coming over soon whether you like it or not."

"Already?"

"Yeah, so let's eat fast and get dressed. What are you gonna wear? Oh, maybe," he says, opening Mara's dresser bewilderingly, "this!" and he throws a light wrapped bag at her so she may catch it.

She rips open the paper and awes, "A Gorillaz T-shirt! I love it," kissing Herman.

"Mara helped me pick it out. We went yesterday while you were sleeping."

"No way! How did she know?"

He raises his eyebrows surprised. "Don't forget to thank her."

"I won't."

Hunger gets to her and they have breakfast on the floor, discussing the odd feeling that plagues Mel every birthday.

"They call 'em the birthday blues," he tells her. "I get them too."

"Strange." She gets cream cheese on her upper lip and has a couple of gulps of fresh squeezed orange juice. "You know, I even had a nightmare about my birthday," she says sweetly through her teeth, ready for the sugar rush.

"Really? What was it?"

"I was at my house—but it wasn't my house." He nods comprehensively. "And all my friends and family were there, but I left them waiting while I found a good outfit. Except I couldn't find one. And I kept trying everything on," her young face wrinkles in sadness, "but nothing was good enough."

She changes into her bathing suit, denim shorts, and new threads, and, forgetting to brush her teeth or wash her face or pee even, she makes an appearance downstairs. Grandma and Grandpa give her a card with a hundred dollars and a pretty wallet to put it in. Carine tells her she'll give her her present later, Wesley and Wes obviously have nothing prepared, and Mara goes, "No problem," when Mel thanks her for the cool tee. Her mother calls some time later and Herman has to make Mel get off the phone or they'd keep talking for hours. The ex wife bitches to him about Mel's sunburnt spots, reminding him to make sure she applies sunscreen correctly, and he hangs up. The Bonhams come over with cupcakes, handing them along to Mel with two twenty-dollar bills in a large clasp envelope.

The Nicchis have a hard time dealing with the Bonhams' insistence on being there early. Herman and Mel both treat it as just something to do, but little by little the twins and their parents get disturbingly vying, gossiping about who's gonna be there and all that. When the timer starts, alone now on their patch of sand, Tilly and Sam push Mel around exactingly.

"No, Mel, this one's lopsided."

"The door collapsed."

"Should you get more water?"

"Five minutes left!"

Mel sighs, hiding her emotions behind her sunflower-shaped sunglasses, her masterpiece a true effort. The judges, three blond moms, walk around the twenty or so groups of eager children. They jot down in shorthand on tiny red notepads while the parents take pictures. One group misses the point and they make a mermaid—a very good one, too—and get disqualified. Some of them are horrible, the competition clearly between four Australian tweens and three boys Tilly and Sam know from school. Someone makes a case for the mermaid people saying they should win for being true artists and thinking outside the box, but no one takes it seriously. Tilly and Sam wait almost angrily for the results, Mel totally over it.

"Ahem," goes one of the blond moms, a paper in her hand. "Hi, all. Thank you for being part of the third annual Santa Monica Children's Sandcastle Building Competition. As most of you already know," and a lot of the parents make some sort of acknowledgement, "I'm Jocelyn Mirren, one of the judges and coordinators along with Amy Ursula and Violet Peterson." The two of them smile daintily. "Parents, I gotta say, I'm really blown away. It looks like everyone did an amazing job." Someone snickers in the crowd. "And I couldn't be more pleased. Each year, they only get better. These kids, I tell ya," and a few of the parents laugh cordially. "So let's get to the point, shall we?" She clears her throat. "Third place and these cool hats go to..." she says, one of the other moms showing a cap to the crowd: 'Santa Monica 2001.' What's it even advertising? "Cole Rapp, and Adam and Jon Brownstein," she reads, clapping. Well, that's not important. They get up to accept their gifts and she moves them aside. "Second place and these hats and four tickets to the Landmark Theater go to...Andrew Wells, Edwin Wells, Caroline Brant, and Adrian Fuller. All the way from Melbourne, everybody." Yeah, yeah, yeah. "And first place..." she makes eye contact with someone specific, "...taking home these awesome hats, tickets to the Landmark, and!" she exclaims, "and three twenty-five dollar Tower Records gift certificates go to...Matilda and Samuel Bonham, and Melanie, uh, Nikki?"

The possibility of winning never occurred to Mel, so when they rush to the prizes, it's one of the first highs of her life. Dad's so proud. He opens his arms as everyone's done clapping, and she rushes to him.

"Hey there, Melanie Nikki," he teases, embracing her briefly.

"I hate it when that happens. Which is—"

"Always, I know. But," he says, taking Mel's bundle of winnings and putting them in his beach bag, "I wouldn't say yours was the best. Those Australians, they...they had it down."

"Don't spoil it," she asks since, maybe, I dunno, it's her birthday and stuff.

And then with a surge of life: "We won!" Tilly bellows in Mel's ear from behind. She takes Mel by the hand and starts sprinting towards the ocean, the wind rustling the red ribbon in her hair. Ahead of them, Sam notices them and begins to jog himself. "We won!"

Not looking where she's going, Tilly's foot catches on a stranger's sunbathing towel, and she almost flies across the hairy man if it weren't for Mel's intuitive pulling of her arm at the last second.

"Come on, loser," Mel jokes around, straightening up to resume their run. She turns her neck and sees Herman and Carine and the Bonhams having a good time. Her feet come into contact with the wet sand and her chest gets all tight. She lets go off Tilly and waves her onward, pressing rigidly over the palpitations. Trying to catch her breath, Mel stays stopped where the water reaches her feet at times. Herman quickens his step and gets to his daughter, asking if everything's okay. "I can't...breathe..."

Faster than he's ever been, Herman takes the beach bag off his shoulder and, knowing exactly where it is, retrieves his own inhaler. He puts it to her face like they've tried a few times before, and she lets the air out first, then places her mouth around the piece, blinking to indicate him to push down.

"Hold it," he instructs, and she nods, doing so. But when she lets the air go, nothing happens. "You need another one?" And so she gets ready for one more puff. Same results. He puts his hands on her shoulders. "Mel, what's wrong?"

With waterfalls, Mel burrows into the cotton on him. She emits a piercing sound without meaning to as he wraps his arms around her, forgetting all his questions.

"It just...it just...hurts."

Breaking his heart for he feels the same, he puts his brow on her neck and lets himself cry as well. All the stress and all the bullshit, they manifest themselves in real tears.

Carine holds Mr. and Mrs. Bonham back by fetching Mara to entertain them with. They ask her about her favorite school subjects and she lies. The twins aren't even in the vicinity. The loud figures on the pier move from one side to the other. A young couple loses control of their cocker spaniel and it sniffs around the two Nicchis intertwined. It helps make them smile.

A long while later, Herman tries to withdraw, but Mel holds on to him. "Remember, it's okay," he says about their weeping, and she moves back, her eyelashes all wet. "Don't be embarrassed."

"But I didn't get hurt," she brings up, thinking that's the rule.

"Sometimes it hurts in here."

"For no reason?" Incapable of being dishonest, Herman nods, standing up. "That's not fair."

"Well, that's life," he says without thinking.

With the pain subsiding, Mel looks for her so-called friends, but by now too much has happened since they were joyous. Good things ruined by bad things always.

They get back to the house, and Grandma shows Mel how she decorated the backyard, except Mel isn't humored. Grandpa keeps behaving like it's any old day by watching TV in the family room. Grandma protests but they're both trying to pretend they're not mad at each other. Sharing a room, in this case the guest room, is proving difficult for the couple that hasn't slept together since Herman and Wesley became adults and left. This last one returns from the grocery store with what Carine asked him, not a single thing missing, pissing off Herman. Wes has a cigarette and Grandma goes berserk.

"I'm eighteen," he makes clear. "O—overage." Mara draws nearer and gets him to call out to her. "Did I miss out on anything?" he asks about the beach. She shakes her head. Carine sees them and orders Mara to step away from the smoke. "See you— ou later."

The party officially starts when Herman gets grilling. The Bonham parents accept Carine's margaritas, the children playing soccer with a water bottle.

"Why don't you have any balls?" Tilly asks Mara.

It sends her brother into a fit of laughter, spilling his coke on himself.

"Samuel Timothy Bonham!" goes his high-pitched mother's voice.

He shakes it off by taking off his T-shirt to put it on inside out and backwards. "There."

"I'm so excited for camp," says Tilly, Sam's name scribbled on his clothes reminding her.

"Eh," he responds.

Wes tries to have a beer but Grandma catches him and throws a fit. Mel tells them to, "Stop! It's my birthday!" yet her lack of patience leads her to storm into the house. Herman gives Carine a look and she understands it's time to bring out the big guns.

"Why don't you come outside?" Carine asks the sulky birthday girl. "There's another present for you."

Mel doesn't really care anymore. She doesn't feel like she deserves it, she doesn't want to deal with what it takes to get it, she'd rather just end the day early. But Carine hangs out close-by with a face that would make anyone feel sorry for her. Giving Mel a lot of personal space, her eyebrows raised as if gifts were worth a person's self-respect, she eventually compels the moppet to just get out there.

"Look who's back!" Herman states bittersweetly. "Come on, open it up."

Shuffling barefoot, soft skin on the rough stone tiles, Mel makes her way to the food table where a box lays in waiting. Everything's become so emotional, getting everyone involved, the limelight watching over her as she rips apart the paper. A flash hits her, the picture being taken seeming redundant when what she got is a Polaroid camera.

"Thanks," she tries to express as gratefully as possible.

But she's sad today. She's just sad today. Carine takes the new gadget out of the box for her—which is totally rude—and tells her to get together with her friends so she may capture the moment forever. The twins barely pay any attention and then hate on the revelation. Mel sets it aside disinterested.

The first burgers are for the imps, and once they're finished—Mel throwing out her paper plate, the others leaving them where they sat—they regroup in the playroom, Tilly and Sam going straight for the shelf containing an immense VHS and DVD collection.

"Have you guys seen *Requiem for a Dream*?" Tilly inquires as Mara turns on the TV. Mel shakes her head. "Our friend's dad gets Academy movies and we watched it and it was..."

"Interesting," Sam concludes for her. "There's this scene in it where two girls do a dildo in the bee-hind."

"What's that?"

Everyone but Mel knows, and they're taken aback by the bluntness. Mara makes a face, Wes another.

"The—the same one?" he asks after a long pause. The twins nod seriously. "So like—" and he makes gestures to explain what he's picturing. It's pretty accurate.

"Would you ever do it in the butt?" asks Tilly.

"Who? Me?" Mara asks in turn. Tilly says yeah, but the casual tone is met by Mara's revulsion. "What is wrong with you?"

"It's supposed to be pleasurable," Tilly teaches her.

"Especially for men," Sam adds.

Mel has no idea what's going on anymore. Mara doesn't know if she can keep up. Wes sits down, his hands on his lap.

"Duuude, you have *The Texas Chain Saw Massacre*? That movie's effed up."

"Never seen it," Mara admits.

"We should watch it," insists Tilly.

"You guys are so weird."

"I—I've seen it," Wes says to Mara.

"Did you like it?"

"Yeah. It's p—p—pretty cool."

"All right," she agrees.

Tilly slides the movie in as Sam turns the lights off. Mara reacts as if she wasn't expecting it, but she's okay with it, Wes sitting next to her on the floor, the little kids on the couch. Mel embeds herself in pillows wishing it wasn't her birthday already. Not knowing how to go about it, she suspires a few times, unable to get anyone's attention.

"Earlier today," Mara begins in a quiet tone, only meant for Wes to hear, "my mom tried to give me 'the talk.'"

"The talk?"

"Yeah, she, like, woke me up early and we were having breakfast and she was like, no sex until you're eighteen, etcetera, etcetera."

"Really?"

"She pisses me off so much sometimes. Like, can you be any more random and awkward?"

"To—o—tally."

"Also, that's some bull crap. Eighteen? Uh, most people lose their virginity when they're sixteen."

"Re—really?"

"I dunno, sounds about right. Except for you."

Sam nudges Tilly. They look at the older two sitting on cushions with their knees up, the energy tense. As the film advances, the twins keep giggling to each other in observance of Wes's arm resting behind Mara, not touching her but for the hairs standing on edge. Fretting that she has onion breath, Mara's already made up her mind that nothing's gonna happen. This can't be her first, well, second impression. The real one. And she's thought about it. Perhaps every second since he got here. Because she's never actually French kissed anyone before. Now would be so easy. Get it over with fast. Who knows if she'll ever get another chance. But no. She couldn't. He's not that ugly, he's not that pretty. Some of it might even be pity. His arm moves half an inch and now they're touching. Both their throats make some sort of noise.

"Just do it already!" Tilly lets out at last.

"Do it!" Sam adds. "Do it!"

Yet as she's about to tell them to settle down, the robust little man, totally out of the Bonham's reassurance, seizes Mara's mouth with his wide lips, his tongue skidding its way into her orifice, engulfing her.

Maintaining her eyes on the screen, Mel ceases blinking, making out the making out in her peripheral vision. The movie gets intense suddenly but not as much as the two heads amateurishly exchanging saliva through obscene sounds. She feels the siblings near her going nuts, fluttering their fingers on each other with unbelievable satisfaction.

"Oh, yeah," Sam whispers in a girlish voice. "Do me good, Wes."

Mara recedes a bit, but Wes puts his thumb to her chin, drawing her nearer.

"Ah, ah, ah," Tilly mutters orgasmically. "It's so big it hurts."

The nerves hit Mara in an unusual way. The carpet under her nails, the hair on her face, a faint static. She brings her arms to her chest, keeping certain things off-hand, only when he keeps reaching around, he senses no resistance. What is it, a bother?

Like she should be ashamed of having limits? What could it be but an inability to say no, and why not? The twins make-believe climax like mobbing capuchins. Wes grabs Mara from the waist and slithers in deeper as his instincts allow him to understand, the girl holding back, the forlorn look in her eyes escaping her sorry mouth with a mewl, drowned out by the twins and their voyeuristic fantasy. Using a rather genteel strength, she pushes him, but his hold is already so firm he might not have felt it. A bit denser now, and he flexes more than he thought he could, one hand reaching for her mouth, the other to his pants. He gives them all a silent moment to change their minds, except Tilly and Sam keep glowing and Mel won't look away from the tube, her eyes shaking before breaking into tears, making for a bleary sight. The jingle of belt, button, zipper. Pulled elastic, proclivity, intrusion. The cherry goes pop and Mel takes her eyes off the television, facing the beast humping on the floor right in front of it. The brightness illuminates the white utter horror of Mara's eyeballs. When she closes her eyes, her eyebrows doing all the work of expressing her feelings, Mel loses her point of reference. She searches from side to side worried it's not what she thinks it is because it's obviously not right. Mara doesn't get to decide these things. And neither do the twins. And neither does Wes. Wes, heaving, pounding, his full weight on the girl, her hipbones poking him in the stomach, her bellybutton suctioning the few hairs of his happy trail, the shoving, the muffled, piercing complaint, and the red light of the switch in the gloom all the way by the door where Mel can't reach without being taken down first. Either way, it's time to try.

Flying with her arms close by her sides, Mel jumps over the sofa and rolls to her knees. At first she's met with laughs, but soon Tilly and Sam wise up and lounge at the sounds of her, incapable of distinguishing anything.

"What are you doing?" Mel spits out as one of them grabs her by the hair. "Ah!" she screams in pain. "Aaah!"

"Shut up!" Tilly orders.

"Get her!" does Sam as Mel frees herself by pushing one on top of the other.

This time, Mel is fast enough. She springs to her feet and gets her hand on the door handle, the other one about to hit the light switch when one of them takes her leg and bites deeply into it. The kid gets kicked in the face as the door opens, letting Mel escape. She closes the door, but it's immediately opened again, Tilly and Sam crawling out of the darkness, keeping the room safe by shutting it away behind their backs.

"No, wait!" Mel realizes, the empty second floor hallway another racetrack of obstacles before reaching the adults. She would never make it, Mara running out of time. And so she throws herself on top of Tilly and Sam, screaming to get back inside. On the other hand, the twins don't move an inch. Wes should be done any time soon. "No! No!" she screeches as loud as her lungs will allow, contracting into tiny breaths that aren't enough to keep her alive.

To their surprise, a pair of footsteps start gingerly from the end of the first floor towards the stairs. All covered in snot, Mel sees an opportunity. Feeling the aghast hands of the twins loosening their grip, she unfetters easily, letting her trip her way down the hall. Herman meets her by Mara's bedroom, taken aback by her frenzy.

"What is it, Mel?" She chokes on the words, not being able to justify her behavior. "Is it your chest again?" She nods but also shakes her head, her nose running down her neck. The new T-shirt, he condemns in his heart, his daughter wiping her face on the sleeve.

"Mara," she sputters. "T—T—Tilly and Sam."

"What about them? What did they do?" He inspects her closer. "Did you do something?"

Tilly and Sam trot in their direction, but as soon as they see Herman, they hurry on back to the playroom, knocking furiously on the door. Suspicious, Herman grabs Mel's hand and leads her to the dillydallying twins.

"Is anything the matter?" Sam asks politely.

"I don't know, is it?"

"Well, we're just watching a movie so you tell me, mister," Tilly responds suavely.

They swing in place playing the innocence card, the room perfectly silent behind them.

"What movie?"

Herman doesn't seem to get it. Mel pulls on his pants with her mouth permanently open in a squarish shape, the drool dripping out the corners, wailing, urgent to speak to her father alone. She stops fast and heavy looking for the right words to explain what is going on, if she even knows, if she's even sure.

"Wes!" she lets out loudly. "Wes! Mara!"

Finally alarmed, Herman eyes Tilly and Sam. He tries to reach for the door and they do their best to not move away. "Excuse me," he has to say, and they, giving each other one last look, separate. Placing a firm hold on the handle, the man opens the door all the way. Mel's heart leaps. The light is turned on. The twins hold their breath. "What's going on?"

Herman stands there for a while waiting for an answer.

"What, Uncle Herman?" goes Wes, his head peeking out from behind the couch.

"What are you watching?

"Uh, *The Texas Chain Saw Massacre*?" the big boy answers.

"*The Texas Chain*—" He looks at Mel. "No, no, no. You kids aren't allowed to—" and he steps forward, approaching the other two. "Mara?"

"Yeah?" goes a wrung voice weakened by exhaustion, remaining unseen.

"Mara, you shouldn't let the kids watch this."

When nothing else happens but Herman keeps staring at them, that's when Mel senses that something's wrong. She inches closer, hiding behind her dad's legs, and peers at the other end where the movie keeps playing. There's Wes sitting with his legs crossed, Mara hunched over hidden by her big hair.

"I'm sorry," she lets out with a squeak. "They insisted. And—and Wes said it was good so..."

Pleased with the situation, Herman steps back and waits for Mel to say anything else, only she continues to shake unreasonably, walking backward in distrust.

"No! No!" she keeps making a fuss, running out of the playroom and down the stairs where she finds Carine on her way in.

"Mel, are you all right?"

"Mara!" she says to her. "Mara!"

"What? What?" the mother flips out.

"Who's crying?" enters Grandma Lisa. "Mel, what is it, dear?"

But all that comes out once again is: "Tilly and Sam! Tilly and Sam!"

"Honey, it's fine," Herman calls out from the second story.

"Mara," Mel repeats to Carine and Grandma Lisa. "Mara."

"Where's Mara?" Carine yells back at Herman.

"She's fine. They're all fine," he lets her know once he reaches them. "Mel, what are you—what's wrong?"

"Mara, Mara."

"Mara!" Carine calls. "Come down here this instant! Did she do anything?" she begins questioning Mel. "Are you okay?"

"Mara, Mara."

This one takes her time, causing her mom to call for her plenty more times, each time more desperately. Yet once Mara gets to the bottom of the stairs, tail between her legs rather uncomfortably, she plays it off well, the bored teenager performance awe-inspiring, her twitching eyelid going unnoticed.

"She got scared 'cause of the movie," Mara lies flatly, curls covering her eyes.

"What the hell are you watching?!" Carine angers, standing in front of Mel protectively.

"It was their fault," she says about the twins as they come down the stairs. "They picked it."

"You're in charge of them—"

"What?! No, I'm not—"

"Do not raise your voice—"

"I'm not raising my voice! You're raising your voice—"

"Go to your room! Now!"

"But I didn't—"

"Mara!"

"Aaaaaah!" Mel roars, startling the whole lot of them. "AAAH!" She grabs a ceramic bud vase from the nearest surface and throws it a long distance onto the wall to reclaim their attention.

"Get a hold of yourself!" Herman commands.

It's still not enough for Carine who, as the other adults start approaching, pleads that Mel: "Quit it!" as if it were that simple.

Hearing this, Herman steps up and attempts to grab Mel, but the wee gal sees it coming, her senses heightened, and makes a run for it once more, this time seeking refuge in the bathroom. Quick after her, Herman reaches the door before she can lock it, and, not realizing he's not being gentle, busts it open, hitting Mel on the head harder than anything. Though his impulse is to apologize, they fight it out until his fingers are almost crushed, giving Mel a chance to shut herself in.

Here she grabs the first breakable thing she finds, the soap holder on the counter, and it goes flying at the wall, making a mess. She does the same with the air freshener, only it clunks and rolls back at her feet. After that she's left with little else to throw besides extra rolls of toilet paper that end up on the floor, it being the half bathroom and all.

"You're gonna have to come outta there eventually!" is the last thing she hears from her father before he stomps away, other feet following him.

Accepting she'll be here for a while, Mel takes a towel so she may sit on the floor against the wall covered up as if it were a blanket. She stops crying and breathes better by the second, her only true wish to be by her mother's side again. Maybe after this he'll want her to go home. She'll make sure to be as difficult as possible.

Not ten minutes go by when a car pulls up to the house. At first she doesn't hear it, but then the bell rings. She stays still, waiting for Carine to open the front door.

"Good afternoon, ma'am. LAPD."

Mel lifts the rail, leaning on the sill, and looks out until she sees, reflected on the next house's living room window, the unlit siren lights of a police car. She can't make out the rest of the conversation because everyone gets stirred up, coming and going with their this and that. In fact, the cops are checking that everything's okay, especially the children—two, three, four of them—after a neighbor called to say they heard screaming.

"I wish they'd come to me directly," she can make out Carine say.

"That's not really how it works, ma'am," one of the policemen responds.

"Well, we're all very close here on this street."

More talking, more walking, and then the front door opens, closes, and the car slowly drives away. She hardly had time to decide to keep quiet. She isn't sure what drove her to that decision, but lately it seems like these ancient institutions of everything sacred are being taken down by the inevitable power of malfeasance. Or something like that.

"What the fug is happening?" she whisper-yells to herself, staring in the mirror. Her pupils rattle in their own pits of misery, that harsh brown evanescing.

Time passes. Slowly as it may, it passes. She blows her nose, picks it, tries snorting water—that's a drug thing, right?—weird stuff, who knows. It's tiresome. A yawn sends her to wiggle her eyelids, the towel rolled up into a ball underneath her head. She never fully drifts into a slumber, but she gets close, an unshakable presence shying her awake. Dread. That dooming sense of becoming airless. Shadow and light flashing in her mind. Tilly and Sam. Mara. Wes.

At some point, when nothing matters anymore, Carine knocks cautiously, giving herself time before letting Mel know that: "Herman's coming."

Unaware of what that entails, Mel sits up in anticipation. The sunlight hits the fair hairs around her knees, the fallow skin smooth under her jerky fingers. She stares at the door straight on. What's he gonna do? Get a key made? Shoot it open? Ha.

"Holy—" she gets caught off guard, the open window met by her father's hands.

In place of acting surprised, she makes eye contact with Herman when he looks inside, figuring out how to climb in. It's a tough one. Doable but barely. Mel dares him to do it. She won't leave on her own, won't back down. If he wants to drag her out, he'll have to drag her out.

"Mel, we can do this the nice way," he says, poking his head in, "or the mean way."

"Don't you mean the easy way or the hard way?"

"No. No, that's not what I mean." She shrugs her shoulders. "All righty then," and he begins his journey in through the rectangle.

Carine comes over and gives him a push, but you can tell she doesn't agree with this. She helps him get past his shoulders, his balding head close to the floor, the flow getting stuck at the hips. Mel sniggers, covering it up with a cough. All that he must do in order to move one inch at a time, his ass crack beginning to show.

"Honey, could you—" but there's not much Carine can do besides push more. As he gets ready to abort the mission, he takes a deep breath, sucking in his belly, and slides the necessary amount to clamber his way onto the toilet.

"Can we just talk? You and me?" Mel asks, trying for the last time.

"You're not gonna talk your way out of this one, Mel. I already called your mom," he says, getting to his feet, gasping for air, grabbing her by the collar. "She's picking you up tomorrow."

A smile crosses Mel's mind, and she doesn't say a thing, at last relieved, willing to get distracted and forget the whole thing happened.

"Look, Her," Wesley comes in on the father and daughter on their way upstairs, "I don't wanna be of any more incon—"

"Just get the fuck out of here," snaps Herman with no time for this.

"I guess then we'll just pack our stuff and—"

"Yes, Wesley! Go! Go!" and he takes the girl stiffly up the steps, her mouth shut peacefully to his dismay. They reach Mara's room. "Pack your stuff," and he blindly opens the door, shoving her inside, the 'Night Mara' sign swinging from side to side.

The sound of it rasping against the wood follows Mel as she faces the three of them in position preying still. Mel doesn't know what to call any of it, Mara in the middle in all her obscure glory surrounded by the hellions thriving in the unusual magic of fast, lamentable situations.

"You know what that means? The sign?" Mara says from her stance on Mel's mattress.

"What?" Mel is daunted to ask. "Night Mara?"

"Yeah." Mel shakes her head. "It's 'cause I'm your biggest nightmare." Even Mel, with her limited vocabulary and lack of sophisticated rhetoric, sees how corny it is, but it also works. Tilly and Sam think about it and find it kind of cool, repeating the moniker under their breath. Having laid that out, Mara begins to pace, chewing on the nails of one hand, then switching to the other. "Did you tell your dad?"

There's peril. It isn't clear what it is, but it's not safe in this room with these people. Mel attempts to focus on the matter at hand, the question, the answer.

"Tell him what?"

"Mara! Mara!" Mara imitates the crying Mel, getting closer.

Mel begins to tremble, her bladder full now that she's not in the bathroom.

"I didn't—nothing happened. Right?"

Studying her from various angles, Mara can tell that she's lying, but she's hoping to see Mel's willingness to stick to it. She sniffs, blanching, the hair sweaty at the roots, puffy at the ends.

"You know you can't tell anyone," Mara says after a while.

"Tell 'em what?"

"I'm serious."

"Yeah," Mel nods, fully dedicated. "So am I."

But Mara's unconvinced. Tilly and Sam grind their teeth, this being the most entertaining show they've ever been a part of.

"I don't know what to do about this, Mel," Mara insists with a heartfelt look. Tilly and Sam share a glance and both raise their hands. "Yes?"

"If you don't wanna get in trouble," Sam begins.

"We," Tilly extends, "think you have only one option."

"What?"

"Well, seeing that Wes is gone and can't confirm or deny..."

"And no one saw anything..." adds Sam, faking concern.

"Since there's no proof for your mom..."

"The only problem being Mel..."

"You're gonna have to get rough."

Mara chews on the idea while Mel swallows.

"Your reasons?" Mara demands, her eyebrows unmoving.

"Well, you're the boss, right?" says Tilly.

"You gotta make sure she doesn't remember," Sam clicks from the side of his mouth.

Everyone takes a beat to gather themselves. It's really, wow, props to the twins, what a great idea. None of them are very familiar with how concussions or amnesia work, but Tilly and Sam seem to have watched the right movies to understand coercion. This alone is enough to make Mara step all the way forward, giving Mel a deadly look. With her eyes, Mel asks her why, if they both know what it is, what's the point of pretending it's something else? Mel isn't foreign to guilt, suffering from decisions others make, being too young, getting corrupted, and whatever else Mara hides in her dogged heart. It isn't pride, is it? No, no, a part of her just vanished to be supplanted by this: a fist, a punch, a dent. And repeat. And repeat. And once again, repeat, more and more and more. The wall and the floor merge into an off-putting angle. One of the baby upper incisors detaches halfway. A cut-out of Tobi Vail on the corkboard twists times ten both clockwise and counter.

"Night Mara! Night Mara!" Tilly begins chanting, getting Sam to join in. "Night Mara! Night Mara!"

Two more pairs of feet, one of them puny, the other huge, get Mel in every spot Mara hasn't already covered. She never gets a chance to stand up for herself, lying there like a pushover. "Be friendly," she heard too many times. "Act nice." And now she takes it, like Mara took it, like Tilly and Sam must inescapably take it somehow. Like Wes.

"Night Mara! Night Mara!"

The adults must think the problem was taken care of, that there can't be any more drama. They must have gotten bored and said yes, thank you, when Carine brought them more margaritas. With Wesley and Wes gone in an instant, Herman is now free to enjoy the big day since, after all, he's turning eight years a father. And he's proven it too. Should the kids get mixed up in any more antics, they'll respect him this time. The sounds of singing reach the backyard. Good. They're playing.

"Night Mara! Night Mara!"

Meanwhile the special one on her special day enters the black for the first time. That one envious of sleep, death's sister, spinal fluid leaking from one place to the other, the tissue rattled round. Not once hit like this before, never to be hit like this again, forever changed by the popular, naïve curiosity of pushing oneself to the limit, that being nothing but pure evil.

19

Lights, ceiling, curtains, beeping, twinges. Nothing. Blinding lights, dropped ceiling, blue curtains, stable beeping, tangible twinges. Nothing. Blinding lights on the dropped ceiling above the blue curtains with a stable beeping marking her tangible twinges.

"Hey there," says a blurry face in scrubs. "Feeling better?"

Traveling thirteen years into the future, she folds her cold arms and reads the wristband: Melaina Nicchi. Voices echo and needles feed. The dream more vivid than her present reality, the heroine sits up, the cables stuck to her tangling up. A clock marks nine forty just as an old man gets rolled in on a wheelchair, already refusing to take off his clothes.

"You have to put on the gown or the doctor won't see you," the nurse lays down.

The blurry face in scrubs appears again and hands Mel her glasses. She holds on to them without putting them on. Besides the infernal headache, her pulse is fast but fine, her blood pressure low but that's usually the case anyway. Her boo-boos, for some reason, have been left untreated.

"Should I tell your boyfriend to come in?" the nurse asks Mel, but this one simply stares back. "I'll go get him."

The nurse goes and returns in long strides, Jameson power walking behind in the worst state Mel's ever seen him in. "What happened? Are you okay?" he starts asking from twenty feet away, trying to leave the nurse behind. "I'm glad they answered 'cause...'" he starts, hoping the nurse will give them some privacy.

"The doctor will be with you shortly," and the nurse closes the curtains halfway, beginning a conversation with the old man's nurse.

"I got locked out," Jameson tells Mel, knowing what she's uncertain about. "I left you my key and then you disappeared. Artie didn't come back either. I had to sleep in my car." Afraid of sounding whiny, he places his hand on her fingers, avoiding the IV. "I kept calling and calling but you never answered. And Artie wouldn't answer either. I even called Pollo. Nothing. I went to your dad's—"

"What?" she asks, but the rate at which she blinks makes it clear that she's probably just asking rhetorically.

"Yeah, I asked him if he knew where you were, said you were no longer his responsibility. I'm sorry to say this, but he did not seem to care at all. I mean, he didn't even know me officially, so I guess that might have crept him out, but I said you had been staying with me. He just said to call your mom, that you had probably gone back to Riverside."

She sits there being caressed as an obese woman gets rushed in, half the staff on her. They yell medical terms back and forth, a devastatingly concerned teenage boy left at the door to wait until it's all sorted out. The way he stands suggests he's been here before. He rubs his face raw with his nails, starting to sweat. He might lose his mother right now. This might be it.

The machine attached to Mel begins making a loud sound.

"Take it easy. Breathe." Jameson advices, smoothing her knotted hair. "Shit, they didn't take care of this?" he asks, looking at her wide-open brow.

With the medicine wearing off, Mel does as instructed, taking a few deep breaths to make the numbers on the screen go down.

"Dr. Sharma," a polished woman says in their direction, going straight for the clipboard at the foot of the bed. "Psychiatry," and she puts her hand out for Mel to shake. Since the patient doesn't respond, Jameson takes it firmly.

"Jameson. Mel's boyfriend."

"So this must be Mel," she says, observing the quick convulsions of Mel's body. "Looking at your chart here, Mel, it appears you were," and she reads from it, "going mad?" She pauses for a long time, and finally Mel nods her head slightly, opening her mouth to breathe. "Anxiety, uncontrollable spasms, hallucinations. Oh my. Were they visual, auditory..."

Confused now that they're not happening, Mel tries to imitate the visions using her hands, looking like someone who's trying to tell another car they don't have their headlights on.

"She's been complaining about it for a few days. She keeps seeing flashes and shadows when nothing's moving."

"Has this happened before?" she asks Jameson, only he doesn't know. "Is she on any medication?"

"Yes! Uh, Wellbutrin and...what's the—oh, uh, Bus...Buspar?"

"Yeah, Buspar. What's it for?"

"Bipolar disorder," he answers confidently. Slyly, Mel does a rolling sign with her index finger. "Rapid cycling," Jameson adds.

"Mh," Dr. Sharma hums. "How long has she been on these meds for?"

"Maybe a month, I don't know. She was taking Lamictal too, but she got a rash from it, and she had to go off it."

"Did she go see her doctor about it?"

"Yeah."

"Because you shouldn't give a bipolar person an anti-depressant without a mood stabilizer."

"That's what I thought! But it's not always the case, right?"

"Psychiatry is an art."

"Is it, though? Or are doctors being marketed? Some free samples here and there. Free lunch, maybe."

Dr. Sharma shrugs, openly disliking the statement. "What she just experienced seems to have been a psychotic break. It's very rare, but some medications have that effect on certain people. I'm gonna recommend she go off the Wellbutrin immediately. No weaning off, just stop. She might be a little moody, but it'll just be for a couple of days," she instructs Jameson. "We gave her something to calm her down, but it should start wearing off soon, so no stress. Just go home and relax. If she can take a few days off, that should help. I'm gonna write her a prescription for Lorazepam, point five milligrams. She should take up to two a day if she needs it. That should get her through the time it takes to get an appointment with a new psychiatrist. Okay?" she says at last, her tone signaling a farewell.

"Thank you so much," he says, making sure to remember all this.

"What about the gunshot wound?" Mel suddenly asks, disorienting them.

"What gunshot wound?" Dr. Sharma and Jameson harmonize.

With a hairy shake of the head, she motions with her hands to forget about it. The doctor gives her some time in case it isn't crazy talk, but Mel seems like she's done with her.

"They'll have her prescription at the door. Hopefully she feels better soon."

"Yeah, thanks," and Dr. Sharma leaves. Jameson closes the curtains and finds Mel's clothes for her as she slowly gets out of bed, ripping off the IV numbly. "Holy fuck! Is that what you meant?" But the tired girl barely looks at him, pulling her jeans on, the ripped denim exposing the bullet graze, a small piece of her thigh missing. "What happened? Why didn't they—"

"It's cool," Mel emits deeply. "Doesn't hurt."

"You're on a shitload of drugs right now."

"Awesome."

"Are you sure—"

"Let's just go," she says impatiently, her mind rearranging the more she articulates her thoughts. "Do you work tonight?"

"No."

"Then can you take me to my—my—my mom's?" she gets stuck, tripping as she puts on a shoe.

"Sure, yeah. Let's go to your mom's," he assents, helping her up.

They grab the prescription and head to the parking lot, the S7 staying behind. She inputs the address on the GPS and plays with the restraint of the seatbelt trying to make herself comfortable, Jameson's bike's tire poking her in the neck. As the ride progresses in silence, the uneasiness slowly returns. Trying to not fluster her, Jameson keeps an eye on her by checking his right shoulder as if to change lanes.

"You told them you were my boyfriend," she says, laughing somewhat.

"Well, when I woke up from my nap, I went ahead and kept calling you more until eventually someone there picked up, and I said that so they would take me seriously and give me the necessary info to come get you. So after a few tries with the goddamn engine," he exhales frustrated, "I got a Rockstar and came straight there."

"Thank you."

"Of course."

"I...I don't know what to tell you," she murmurs.

"You could start with what happened."

"I don't...I'm not...give me a minute."

"You don't actually have to explain anything. I'm just glad you're okay."

"No, but...I...I think I remember everything."

"What everything? The whole—"

"Night Mara."

"Night Mara?"

"You're gonna feel awful about your band name."

"What? Why?"

Still fighting with the breast crushing seatbelt, Mel makes a joke about having boobs before telling him what she remembers from the last twenty-four hours, mostly just the consternation of waking up in the middle of the night on the floor of a strange house with her hands tied, a bump on her head, a vase at her feet, locked bedrooms farther in, making no mention of the attempt on Pollo, the money, Celeste's demise, no, none of that. These are mere dizzy pieces masking the facts incoherently outside of herself. Unreal.

Other cars passing him, Jameson encounters the end of Mel's story. He wasn't ready for that. If anything he imagined she had a fit and went off running like the capricious often do. He had no idea if her things were still in his room or not. But then again, she could have gotten into serious trouble. He wasn't sure yet how responsible or lucky she was, seeing her dead on every dark sidewalk as he drove around trying to find her. He tried to unlax thinking she'd come back unscathed, teasing him for caring so much. When the hospital answered and said they had her, he figured she must have overdosed on something, and that was a horrifying thought but at least she was being taken care of. It didn't have to be this.

"When does it end?"

"What?"

"The abuse," he tells her. "Century after century, father to son, everywhere always...I mean, look at us. Even us, and we're good people. We don't have it that rough when you think about it. And still you're fucked up, god fucking knows I'm fucked up...Artie's fucked up—"

"Well—"

"No, you don't even know half of it. Artie and I were really good friends at some point so—not to defend her or anything, like, I don't know how she can be my in my life after this—but she...that family...her dad...her mom! And don't forget Pollo. I fucking hate that guy."

"Sam."

"Yeah, huh?" He rolls down the window a tad to burp out of it without Mel noticing. "You know, I always had a suspicion that I could never confirm, but now, maybe, maybe it explains something. Maybe that's why she changed her name," his eyes go into space. "Yeah. Yeah, yeah, she must have changed it so they wouldn't have the same name."

"What do you mean?"

"Artie, she...she looks and sounds like a slut and all, but she never actually has sex with any guys, nothing. Unless she keeps it on the way down low, but even then...she's—she's not that kind of person.

"Oh, no," Mel utters, her lungs contracting. "You think maybe they..."

"Could be."

"That's too much."

"Or maybe she just wanted to reclaim her identity, I dunno. Don't people get stupid tattoos to remind themselves they've overcome something?"

"She got a whole new face! Although, who knows. Who's got the time to be psychoanalyzed? But...I don't wanna talk about it anymore," Mel states, picking at her neck. "I just wanna go home."

"Twenty more minutes."

They turn taciturn while the morning traffic clears up on the 60, "Subterranean Homesick Blues" playing on the radio. Mel gets ready by finding the key to her mother's house in her giant purse. Her hand comes across the Polaroid and it sends shivers down her spine. When they get to the cul-de-sac and enter the clean, quiet house and use the bathroom, serve themselves orange juice, and sit down to watch TV, Mel takes her mom's tablet and logs onto Facebook. It takes her a few tries—different spellings and some extra letters—before she gets it right, but there she is: Isamara Courtenay.

Mel's stomach starts rumbling, so she sets the tablet aside. "I'm gonna take a quick shower," she tells Jameson. He picks another *Sunny*, and by the time the name of the episode is revealed, he's already dreaming he's part of the show.

20

"Why didn't you tell me you were coming?"

Stunned, Jameson opens his eyes all the way without moving his body.

"I texted you!"

"I didn't get anything."

A short red-haired lady in her fifties carrying two reusable bags stops and stares at the scruffy man on her couch. Mel appears from behind and takes the bags to the kitchen.

"This is Jameson," Mel says out of sight. "He drove me."

"Well, thank you, Jameson. I've missed this girl," and she nods in Mel's direction as soon as she's back. "What's with your face?"

"Nothing," Mel fibs, patting her band-aid collage.

"What happened?" she asks with worry. "And why are you limping?"

Mel frowns, shaking her head, waving it away. "It's nothing. How are you?" she changes the subject ungraciously.

"Fine," her mother accepts without wanting to, eyeing Mel. She goes around the lamp and shakes Jameson's hand. "Socorro."

"Jame—"

"Son, yes," she wraps up for him in an inimitable accent, shifting back to Mel. "¿Todo bien?"

"Yeah."

"¿Segura?

"¡Sí!" Mel erupts.

"Easy," Jameson says to her, rising to his feet to grab her by the elbow and lead her to sit. "Uh, ma'am, she can't be agitated."

"And why not?" Socorro accuses, waiting for Mel to give in and—

"I had a psychotic break," she ultimately sighs. "Psicosis."

"¿Cómo?"

"But it's fine, it was just some medication I was taking."

"And now you're off it."

"Yeah, takes a few days."

Socorro bites her lip, clearly used to these kinds of things. "Are you guys hungry?"

Neither of the youngsters replies heartily, yet she still throws together two bomb-ass paninis and a strawberry-banana smoothie.

"So, uh, Dad kicked me out."

"When?!"

"Ye...yesterday?" she asks desynchronized, trying to get confirmation from Jameson. He blinks once.

"Why?!"

"I honestly don't know. Oh, maybe 'cause he's fucking nuts. Bipolar piece of shit. The motherfucker just takes Valium. As if life were that easy."

"Do you have your things?"

"Most of them are at his place," and Mel points at Jameson. "He lives a few apartments away from Herman. But I couldn't get everything out. There's still some stuff I need to—"

"Mel!" Socorro says, raising her voice. "What happened to your leg?!"

"Mom!"

"Ma'am."

"Sorry." Socorro crosses her arms. "Every time you come back from your dad's, there's something wrong with you."

"I don't plan on...being family anymore," Mel concludes, getting up to use the bathroom, taking the tablet with her. She pees and clicks on Mara's profile. Dartmouth class of '11, situated in Los Angeles, and a picture of her rock climbing. Against her better judgment, she pays a dollar for a short, un-revised message to get to her main inbox. Before regretting it, she sets the tablet down, wipes, pulls up her pants, flushes, and washes her hands, gearing up for all the possibilities that may now unfold.

Leaving Jameson to his nap on Mel's bed, Socorro takes Mel to the pharmacy to get the Ativan. "As fast as you can, please," Socorro says to the pharmacist, throwing a side glance at Mel grinding her teeth, her body temperature fluctuating in an extra large AC/DC T-shirt. They wait around for ten minutes idling down the magazine aisle, then Mom pays and Mel pops three straight up.

"I don't mean to throw in the towel so soon, but it's okay if I come back, right?" Mel inquires on their way back home.

Socorro doesn't respond, offended by the question. "We need to find a new psychiatrist."

Knowing her mother will take care of that for her, Mel excuses herself saying, "These pills are making me hella tired," and goes to her room where she rolls Jameson towards the wall, making some room on the queen-sized bed. Her whole history plays out of order in her head as soon as she shuts her eyes, marking the crow's feet that'll one day show. All she needs now is some closure.

21

A full bladder bothers Mel to the point where she can't, she just can't anymore, forcing herself to lucid her way out of forgettable nightmares and use the bathroom. Must be the polyuria again. She grabs her phone and checks it once she's got a flow going, halting when she reads a text from a 310 number: *hi mel, i got your message. i'd love to grab some coffee and catch up. i'm free from twelve to one every day during the week if you wanna meet up. i work in encino on ventura and woodley. let me know what works for you. - mara.*

Furious that her fingers can't type fast enough, Mel sends her back: *what about this tuesday?*

The thought of staying up occurs to Mel, but once she sees Jameson with his face all puffy on the pillow, she gets back in bed and helps him turn on his other side. He becomes conscious for a few seconds and gives her his cheek to kiss. Mel holds him, exhaling moistly on the nape of his neck. His skin smells like a sunset in a breezy room atop a skyscraper. Since she can't sleep, she walks along the hardwood floors barefoot. Having no trouble biding her time, she goes ahead and closes the bow windows. Once she's done, she sits in the middle of the room and there's total silence. She crosses her legs and begins to drift...

The cell phone rings. Excited, she has no problem sitting up, Jameson grunting, to check what it is: *you mean today? because today really works for me. let's meet at coffee bean at noon.*

Mel looks at the date on her phone and can't believe she slept through a whole day. Jameson, too, the poor bastard. He might have taken some Ativan himself, or maybe she dreamt it, who knows. She checks the time to make sure it's that tight before tapping Jameson on the shoulder.

"Baby," slips out of her mouth, scratching his beard so as to get it stuck inside her fingernails—oh what a feeling. "Jaaamesooon...time to wake up." He avoids her as much as he can until she starts touching his dick, then he can't hide a smile. "I really need to ask you a faaavooor," she sings for him.

"Well, I just might grant it to you," he grunts, keeping his eyes closed.

"Can you drive me to Encino, like, right now?"

"Right now?"

"Aha."

"Why? What's there?"

"The one and only...drum roll please," and he duplicates a snare. "Night Mara."

"What? You're meeting with her?"

"Yup. We've been texting."

"All this happened while I was asleep? I took two of your things, by the way. Figured you wouldn't mind."

"Yeah, no problem."

"I just didn't wanna be awake while you were still sleeping. Your mom's cool, though. We had dinner and watched *The Sopranos* together."

He yawns, tearing up, while she gets dressed a bit more elegantly, choosing a T-shirt without holes in it, white socks, the backup Converse. She even brushes her hair and puts on mascara. Not that it makes her look any less insane, her face all shades of pale and purple, the limp apparent. A flash crosses the corner of her eye, the first one since leaving the hospital. It brings everything else with it, slapping Mel in the face for acting like nothing happened. Her eyes getting wobbly, a crooked grin takes her face by surprise.

They count change at the gas station and the guy let's them take their two energy drinks ten cents short. Mel pays for Jameson's tank of gas with her credit card, and soon they're hurrying to the San Fernando Valley. "We'll make it," Jameson keeps saying, the Cavalier emitting all sorts of sounds when he takes it to sixty. Mel holds on to her watch, covering it to remain tranquil. This method, however, proves useless once Jameson takes the car one lane at a time towards the shoulder as they reach Arcadia, feeling the car giving up somewhat, exiting the freeway before it's too late. He gets out and stretches while searching in his wallet for his AAA card, if he has it, trying to pretend Mel isn't doing a poor job of hiding her hot, desperate tears, her hands rubbing a tissue against the dark circles under her eyes.

"Get an Uber," he insists as he's put on hold for roadside assistance, knowing Mel has no trouble wasting her money on luxuries. "And take a pill."

Nodding, she gives him one too and they swallow them down with warm water from the car, a driver already on the way. They say goodbye without any clear plan of how they'll reunite. She waves at him from behind the window as the tow truck pulls up. They'll figure it out. They have a lot of things to figure out.

Halfway there, she is officially late. Traffic doesn't help starting from Glendale all the way to Sherman Oaks, but Mel sends Mara a pretty accurate ETA, and so even when her desperation overcomes the drugs, her palms sweating out of control, she isn't rude when, forty minutes into Mara's lunch break, Mel rushes in, her legs floundering once she finds the twenty-five-year-old version of that girl from forever ago.

Popping another Ativan real quick, she makes her way through the crowd pussying out in scarves in the biting Southern California November, approaching the unsuspecting Mara requesting a refill. She pays with her smart phone before Mel takes on bravery and says: "Hello."

A long second goes by before the look of recognition becomes her, giving Mel a broad smile and a small hug. "Hi there," Mara says softly, her Native American earrings making the finest dangling chimes.

From the get-go, Mel sees that Mara hasn't kept up the punk rock essence that was such a paramount aspect of her persona. She's in a trendy blue jacket from Bebe or something, a faux leather purse on one shoulder, keratin vanquishing her wild hair boring, all prim and proper.

"How's your mom?"

"Better, better. Her diabetes was a bit out of control for a while, but now she's better, much better. How's Herman?"

"Ugh, don't get me started," Mel gibes, but Mara doesn't like it. "So you work here?"

"Yeah, in that building," Mara tells her, pointing behind her. "I just started this year. I'm still working on my master's. Psych. It took me a while to decide what to do, you know? I was going to school for business, but even though it wasn't easy to come to that conclusion, at the end of the day, I realized it just wasn't my thing. And that was when I switched majors and all my problems ended," she states proudly. "Now I'm focusing on troubled youths. I started going to juvie and low income neighborhoods and all that."

"Mara!"

A small coffee is served, but Mara doesn't hear it, forcing Mel to distract her from her fascinating life story and point it out to her. She blows into it through the hole on the lid, then takes a sip while trying to ignore Mel's prominent sulk, the stoned stare, all those injuries. Mel moves up to the register and orders an iced coffee with soy milk, pays with her card, then stands around to wait for it while Mara adds honey and cinnamon to her hot drink.

"Last thing I heard of you was you were heading off to Sarah Lawrence. I think our moms are friends on Facebook."

"Yeah," Mel accepts. "It's been years."

"We're not family anymore."

"I'm sure everyone was better off in the end."

"What are you talking about? Herman was like a father to me," Mara contradicts her.

"Lucky you."

"Yeah, lucky me, I got to live through another divorce." Once Mel gets her coffee, they find a place to sit. Mara removes her purse, then checks her cell phone. "Are you still living in, uh...?"

"No, I'm currently in Ventura."

"Boulevard?"

"County."

"Never been there."

"There's no reason to."

"What are you doing there?"

Her questioning is the right amount of polite and phony, somewhat expecting to speak herself like she's got more to brag about. This is exactly the part Mel's not interested in.

"I had some, uh, health issues. Had to take some time off. Decided to try living with Herman a bit. You know, to save," Mel glosses over. "What about you? You look so different."

"You look the same," Mara laughs, disregarding how her comment makes Mel jump a little in her chair, hitting her ribs on the table. She repeats it a few more times just to herself, then keeps talking about her job and studies, checking her phone every few minutes—rude, don't you think?—making it clear that when the time comes, she's just gonna leave and go on with her life. "'Choose a job you love, and you will never have to work a day in your life' kinda thing," she keeps going.

Mel slurps the remainder of her drink, her oral fixation running out of things to do. She waits for Mara to take a breather, yet she chats like she and Mel were still sisters, close sisters, comfortable enough to be sincere hopefully.

"Look, Mara—"

"Yes, yes, you messaged saying you had something to ask me. Go ahead. If you don't stop me, I'll just ramble on."

"You didn't use to be so talkative."

"You're still pretty quiet."

"I only speak when I have something to say," Mel states, not knowing whether it's true or not. "Anyway, I...shit, where to start," she says mostly to herself, pressing on her temples. "Actually you might be able to help me."

"Ooh, with what?"

"I, uh, think I have PTSD or something. I've no idea how to make myself sound less deranged, but..." Mel begins, bracing herself. "There's just something that's been bothering me. I, uh, I guess you could say I suffer from depression," she says, looking to see if she can find something of the kind in Mara's stare, but she blinks rapidly in anticipation. "It's all very hard to explain, but, uh, I recently had some trouble unveiling some truths, and it was all just really strange..." Mel drags on, unsure of how to go ahead and ask her. Meanwhile, Mara withdraws an inch, then another, her confusion hardening. "Do you remember that summer when I was eight, you were twelve, and I came over to your mom and dad's house?"

A hint of consternation colors Mara's face maroon, but she lets on nothing. It's tender how it happens, really. Here someone thrives in the controlled environment of their own ideas, protected at all times, about to confront what is probably disguising those lying eyes. Using the correct nomenclature sharpens the lines otherwise blurred by the desire to undo and the cowardice of covering up. You don't let her become a stripper, a teen mom, a crack addict, but that doesn't repair her any less broken. It's always in the eyes—whatever you're looking for, that's where you'll find it—and Mara has the wettest, honey dripping abyss of caving hazel eyes, Mel thinks absentmindedly, missing the straw. When she gets to it, she sucks in all the ice water.

"Barely," Mara ultimately answers. "Were you there all summer?"

"I don't think so, no. Trip ended early, you could say."

"How's that?" she defends herself, feigning interest.

"I got really hurt," Mel confesses.

"Oh. I'm sorry to hear that."

Mara sets the coffee down before her, cracking her stubby fingers, light bouncing off the gold ring on her pinky. Mel copies this behavior, her knuckles more strident. Moving her cup aside, she shakes her head, frustration adumbrating her demeanor.

"What's with this shared notion that I don't know? Why does everyone assume I'm stupid?" Mel blurts out, losing her cool. "Do you really believe in taking a secret to the grave? Come on, Mara, we were just kids."

"Exactly," Mara exhales, bringing the tone down. "So what does it matter now?"

"You realize things are different nowadays, right? It's not bad manners anymore to be honest about what happened to you."

"What happened to me? I thought we were talking about what happened to you."

"You beat me up, Mara, who gives a shit? You got raped," Mel lets out, doing her best to keep it low.

The sound of those last words build their way into being, and after they settle, it's done. Mel might put her hand to her mouth, but there's no taking that back. Mara lets it sink in, looking around to make sure most people are wearing headphones, responding with a tiny laugh, protecting the monster that feeds on her.

"Is that what they're calling it now?"

"What do you mean? You were a child—"

"I wasn't a child. I knew perfectly well what I was doing. "

"You were twelve," Mel maintains.

"I was pubescent."

"Are these the things..." you tell yourself? Mel finishes in her head. "Never mind. I'm way out of line."

"Yes," the other one agrees, taking a large gulp of coffee with it. "Yes, you are."

"I just wanted to leave it all behind me. It's been holding me back."

"You sure you don't wanna get your story straight first?"

"You're gonna tell me a twelve-year-old girl knowingly and willingly had sex with an eighteen-year-old man and there's no crime there? Not even in the least bit?"

"I grew up fast, Mel. It was the nineties," she jokes, but Mel doesn't find it funny, especially since she gets the wrong decade. "There's a lot you never knew about me. Never had the time to find out. Just like I don't know practically anything about you."

"That's not what this is about," Mel reminds her.

"Did you know that your own father was almost molested? Yeah, he told me in confidence. When he was little he got into an old man's car with the promise of an ice cream, but as soon as the man put his hand on his lap, he got afraid and ran away."

"But that's not what you did."

Regretting it immediately, Mel lowers her gaze to let Mara scoot her chair back, their rendezvous slowly turning into a scene.

"You know, I could get really offended and just walk away right now."

"I'm sorry, I just—there's no right way to go about this. I had a goddamn psychotic break 'cause of these fucking meds I was taking and I...I fucking lost my mind. I—I remembered that summer...I was trying to remember, I was trying really hard, and I guess the pain...I dunno what it was. The mere thought of a repressed memory makes me feel all," and it happens, "claustrophobic and I—I—I don't know what to do now. It's been affecting me my whole life without me knowing it. I'm—I'm..."

As tears begin to form in Mel's eyes, she looks up one last time at Mara before letting her hair fall over her face, and in that quick connection, Mel coming undone, Mara holding her head high, they share compassion back and forth.

"Mel," says Mara, her eyelid twitching. "This isn't necessarily the best environment to have this conversation, but if any of my work is relevant, then just know this: good exists. It's really easy to see the evil in the world, but finding goodness, that's what matters."

"That's what all therapists say," Mel sniffles. "You have to change your outlook on the world, blah blah blah."

"It's not blah blah blah. It's true. You can take all the meds you want, but negativity, that's in your own heart."

"So you're saying you got over it by being positive," Mel alleges, bringing the conversation back to her original point.

"Sure," Mara exhales, not wanting to admit to Mel's version of what happened.

"I find that approach overly demanding."

"I'm trying not to tell you to go fuck yourself, okay? You think you can just show up in someone's life and tell them they're— I...I really can't believe this. I mean, come on, I should have left already."

"But you pity me. And now you're giving me the best advice you can because you know I'm right, and it's gonna take me perhaps years to come to terms with the fact that when I was a child, I witnessed a—a—a rape...and then I was beaten up about it. Great. I'll just do yoga and juice kale and get a fucking GMO dog and everything will mend itself. Maybe if I write down three positive things that happen to me every day before going to bed, I will one day wake up without depression. Or maybe I should check my Vitamin B levels. My thyroid. Switch to progestin-only birth control—"

"What are you trying to prove?"

"That the lie is probably so engrained in you that you can't even see—"

"And if that was the case, so what? You're gonna come here and tear down the whole defense mechanism I've built for myself? What gives you that right?"

"I just want the truth, dude."

"What for? Didn't you say you remembered?"

"If I can forget a whole episode of my life, then I am not trustworthy."

"Well, I'm sorry you're just now having to face your problems."

"Problems? Traumas, Mara. Traumas. I saw something horrible and I couldn't do anything to stop it. You know how that feels? I really wish you'd take me seriously here—"

"Trust me, I'm being as professional as my dignity allows."

Defeated, Mel blows her nose vehemently, putting the used napkin in her pocket while Mara finishes her drink.

"Wes died."

"I know."

"For the guy who took your virginity, you don't sound too moved."

"Would you care if your first died today?"

"Touché."

Mel gets ready to unload more on her when Mara enters Mel's personal space and grabs her wrist, checking the time.

"Sorry, but I gotta go."

"Yeah, all right."

"If you wanna talk more, do let me know. If I'd known what you were up to, I would've offered a better setting."

"It's cool. Keeps me in check. Next time I'll just make an appointment."

"That's funny," Mara says without the slightest hint that it was. "But hey, if you do need to find someone, I know plenty of great shrinks around here."

"Thanks."

"Aha," and she gets ready, fumbling with her things. "I wish you the best. I really do. I'm sorry you're going through a rough time."

"It's fine, I'm used to it."

On that note, Mara gladly stands, putting her hand on Mel's shoulder for a second. It seems like she's about to apologize, that seventeenth of June becoming more vivid, until she concludes that she doesn't have to. She utters an airy farewell and simply scuds back to work, knowingly leaving Mel worse than before. Not her problem. If she's learned anything about mental disease, that would be to stay the fuck away from batty people's drama once it starts to affect you. Sometimes you gotta take care of yourself first.

The memories, though, they contend with her serene scene, the elevator two floors away. Finding herself unaccompanied as she goes up six stories, Mara's eyelid begins to quiver more visibly, rendering her useless for the rest of the day. She's hoping there's a chance she can postpone all her work, skip that class at USC later, not go to the gym. She'll say it's a migraine since everyone's aware she gets bad ones from time to time, frankly feeling one coming on. And so she gets to the office and tells Rita she's not feeling well, saying she needs to lay down in the conference room undisturbed for a while.

Shutting the blinds, Mara leaves the busy street downstairs, evading her reflection on the glass of a print of Eva Bonnier's *Magdalena*. She takes off her boots and sits on one of the rolling chairs with her knees up, burying her head between her legs, the songs from back in the day getting stuck in her head all at the same time. Girl power. Sex. Violence.

Breaking down for once in years, Mara revisits Mel's agony as if it wasn't hers. After all, the pricey education she received in the field was supposed to help. She doesn't know why she chooses this route, but it would be inconvenient to choose the one Mel suggested. And what would be the point? Everyone would do their best to sympathize, and then their opinion of her would inevitably change for the worse. Nobody wants to be victimized. Like killing the woman rather than letting her live a life of shame.

But why? She never even saw it happen, lying there refusing kindly, eventually falling unresponsive as long as he needed her to. The hasty knocks on the door gave him another few seconds, the risk exciting him enough to come. Mara was already aware that you can't actually feel it happening inside, but she's pretty sure she did. Wes's face creased in ways his age didn't have a chance to see fit, moaning like an animal. He jolted one last throe and didn't waste any time before withdrawing, making sure to conceal his weapon. "Come on, go!" he commanded, and she obeyed, redressing the pants-free leg, semen leaking out of her, sticking to her underwear. Herman eyed them with care, but Mara merely took the nagging while Wes whispered something in his father's ear. An hour later, the pair ditched the party. It must have been the cops who showed up to check on the children that made him leave. Or, really, the way Mara froze when one of them asked her if she was all right. That must have been it. But Mara never told a soul. She finally had intercourse in college, and that's what she counted as her first time. It hardly ever satisfied her. Her roommate was assaulted when she passed out at a frat house, and she cried on Mara's shoulder many a night, each time congealing Mara's decision to keep her secrets to herself, disgusted by how her peer made her feel. And now she's been subjected to feeling that way again, only this time about herself, making her question everything. Just like Mel intended.

Fucking whore with her hipster glasses sitting there expecting what exactly? What was even her question? Oh, excuse me, were you, um, raped in front of me? No. No, I'm not some sociopath incapable of loving. Not a whore seeking validation. Eternally twelve-years-old. Quite the contrary. Hear that? The birds are chirping. La la la. Right?

Sneaking up on her with all the hatred she's ever felt, Mara holds her breath. A tear gradually escapes her eye. She lets it drop down her cheek before wiping it off. Okay, she grieved. Now it's time to move on.

She makes an effort to stand up, but another tear weakens her back on her buttocks. Sure, maybe one more is fine. But don't you start crying now, sweet baby. It was no fault of yours. You may have flirted, you may have teased, but what you got was in no way what you were in it for. Maybe you, too, preferred to erase the suppressed supplications, the hundred and sixty pounds of mass, the hitchhiker slicing his hand open in the travelers' van. The last girl makes it out alive in the end, but Mara didn't stick around to find out. If she had, she would have identified with the survivor. Then again, doesn't it make you think what kind of life she could have lead after the massacre?

Mara didn't ask herself these questions. She resolved to subdue Mel in order to save her ass, and it balanced out her actions. Morally, not once did Mara feel a burden about that. It shouldn't automatically make her a bad person. Besides, that's just how it works. Someone does something to you, you take it out on someone else, and it gets passed on, stealing irreplaceable parts of a human being half on purpose, the other half supposedly not. All throughout history, every single kid marred into devolution, reproducing, mutating, just to get to this point where only a minority gets to enjoy the sumptuous life of growing up healthy.

A black cloud embraces her as she reconsiders. This was not her plan for today. Mostly she figured Mel was gonna ask her for money, totally plausible given her notorious personality. Instead, Mel showed to be way past that, enthralled by the morbid. Contagious as it is, Mara attempts to recall something heartwarming, a joke, a show tune, whatever. No matter what, the dread gets to her, consuming her from head to toe. What did you think? That an individual can be better than that? You don't get it. Death taints all but beautiful death itself, and in a world where everyone's afraid of dying, you gotta find something to kill. Try and recover your goodness now, Night Mara, right here, right now. Psychedelics would help, a Patronus, Lacuna. But instead of working towards alleviating, the energy jumbles up her past, more recent actions contributing to her earlier punishment, backwards karma, the way she was affected, the person she became, every little embarrassing moment, any speck of selfishness, whenever she didn't admit to something, amended by the world's yin-yang. Yet as much as she'll deal, drinking herself into the toilet, attempting to want to get laid, buying a bunch of shoes, lifting weights, making advances in her research, however she deals with it, there's no avoiding the better day that will come. And it's not because she deserves it. Life doesn't work that way. It's because she fucking wants it. Happiness is usually inherited anyway. Thanks, Mom and Dad.

The hours pass and everyone leaves by four. Mara sneaks out unnoticed and sits in her car for a while. Her angel and devil fight it out, and guess which one she chooses.

If she doesn't leave now, she won't make it to her class on time. Then she'll go to the gym, and on the way back, she'll pick up something from the Ralphs deli. She'll sign into her HBO Go app on her smart TV after a shower, and that will take care of her falling asleep. She doesn't tend to dream so there's nothing to get distressed over. Tomorrow she'll wake up at seven, she'll do her hair and makeup, listen to the radio, hit up Coffee Bean, check her e-mail...

Romina D'Alessandro was born in 1992 in Montevideo, Uruguay. She now lives in Southern California where she works for a living.

www.nightmaranovel.com

@wheninromina

www.ingramcontent.com/pod-product-compliance
Lightning Source LLC
Chambersburg PA
CBHW071324250626
47159CB00004B/1451